The Composure of Butterflies

Te'yana Pugh

Copyright © 2024 by Te'yana Pugh
©Forward Canary&Sage Publishing

Printed in the United States
Book Cover by Te'yana Pugh
Illustrations by Te'yana Pugh
ISBN: 979-8-218-36483-0
10 9 8 7 6 5 4 3 2 1

The Composure of Butterflies

The moonlight crept in just as gently as the darkness, and now, the Woman knows why wolves howl at the moon, and why lovers, like moonflowers, wait for the stillness of the night just to dance beneath it.

DR. MURPHY

"I think you're perfect for it, Bennette. Really!" she said the day before he left. Her eyes shifted quickly from left to right as she tried to imagine being inside of their home without his presence. Bennette recognized the flushing of her cheeks, and the crooked smile that slowly formed across her face immediately after he told her the news. Bennette accepted the offer to become the new head chef at a booming restaurant in Argentina and would be gone for the entirety of the semester.

She stood before him trying to understand why she had said "yes" the day he dropped to one knee to propose. It was obvious that the two of them rushed into it, and because of this, their marriage could be compared to a theatrical play. With each of them playing the deuteragonist in each other's lives.

"Don't be so disappointed!" Bennette said to her. Dr. Murphy had forgotten to mask, to appear as a damsel in distress, a woman entirely lost without the comfort of his presence. To feed his ego she responded with more concern.

"I don't think we've ever been away from each other this long. Who's going to make me dinner?"

Bennette threw a pillow in her direction. "That's all I am good for, huh?"

Yes, yes, that is it really. Seven years in. Space would do us both some good, and you know it.

Dr. Murphy thought to herself before answering him. "Of course not!"

That was two weeks before and now Dr. Murphy sat near the window and watched as the birds below dug their beaks into a nearly dead patch of grass. It was the first day of a semester without Bennette and the very first semester she'd lecture to a classroom in which only five women had elected to join. She fought tooth and nail for the dean, who wanted to cancel the course on account of low enrollment, to keep it open. For the occasion Dr. Murphy chose to wear a blazer, something Bennette had become quite fond of, simply because the blazers she wore were often his.

"A bit of me wherever you go," he'd say, before eventually the conversation would result in sarcastic banters on the rare occasion, they'd want to wear the same one.

"I had it first, woman!"

"It looks better on me!" Dr. Murphy teased, and Bennette would agree.

"You're right, your shoulders are much larger than mine, linebacker!"

A thickly lined blazer, sometimes paired with wide leg trousers, was a sure way to find her inner confidence; being afforded the ability to oscillate between masculinity and femininity through clothing was worth taking advantage of. The blend of masculine and feminine energy always made her feel more balanced. It always had, for even as a teenager, she went through the men's section at thrift stores in search of the perfect pieces.

There at the window, Dr. Murphy smirked, because with Bennette away to Argentina, she could wear whichever items of clothing he left behind.

Looking at the time, Dr. Murphy quickly stood, she was running late. She had spent the better part of the morning turning the pages of a paperback anthology and romanticizing everything that might transpire during the upcoming semester. Time escaped her, but still, she was prepared. Little did her new students know she had already studied their transcripts and asked their previous professors about their ability to be studious. Knew which student was a repeat. Dr. Murphy knew what each of their majors were, too. While some professors walked into their classrooms unthinkingly, leaving the culture of the class to chance, she always took it upon herself to do research at the beginning of each semester.

KAT

The evening that Kat's boyfriend was expected to visit her she needed her children to go to bed on time. However, the two of them only played, behaving as if she had not stood beside them, and asked them to obey several times over. But it wasn't until she, freshly showered, slipped on the toy train her son left behind that she screamed the cruelest words she'd ever spoken to him.

"I WISH I NEVER HAD YOU!"

"I'd never wish it on my worst enemy!"

Motherhood. She had no energy for bedtime stories, for preparing meals, nor did she have the desire to interact childishly with her children. To play. In fact, she found it painfully amusing that she never knew what she wanted until it was too late, like being intimate with a man to escape herself, or having the child that she wished she'd aborted. An endless cycle of self-sabotage that she had no doubt learned from her own mother.

Kat loved her children but regretted them with every inch of her tired body. Wanting nothing more than to be alone, she preferred to be hidden in her bedroom, curtains drawn in absolute darkness. Being alone was never an option in motherhood. *What was I thinking?* she thought when everything began to feel too much.

Though, there were some good days, and moments that the terrible days made her forget. The days in which she'd get out of bed and make homemade French toast or pancakes, go to the park, with wide eyes—the three of them in search of fairies. She'd read to them before bed and lay beside them until they fell asleep, but mostly it was all terrible.

Triggered, she let her true feelings escape from her mouth *that* evening, which she remembered vividly, her words were sharp, and stung like tiny self-inflicted paper cuts that made her lips tremble.

I fucking hate you; I hate you so fucking much! An unhinged version of herself screamed on the inside.

Afterwards, her son looked up at her with his big blue eyes. He was both emotionally wounded and confused. In pain, Kat stood up, and spoke to him in the way she should have at the very beginning, with kindness and patience.

"I am sorry baby, Mommy didn't mean to yell," she said, naked, ignoring the water that dripped from her mother-ish body. Her son wrapped his bony legs around her waist and rested his head on her shoulder.

"Are you ok?"

The boy nodded.

"Do you want ice-cream tomorrow?" another nod.

"Ok, well, if you want ice-cream, then you have to be good, you have to pick up your toys and take a bath. You must go to sleep," she said before sitting him down. Her mood then at once changed from nurturing back to cold.

"Ok, mama, I am the baby?" he asked, looking at her with genuine concern.

"Yes, you're the baby, and you're a good baby," Kat said, rubbing her shaking fingers through his hair, forgetting for a moment that she had another child that was "A baby" too.

Satisfied with his mother's answer, the boy picked up his toy train and ran into the bedroom while Kat grabbed a towel, looked at her reddened body in the mirror, and cried.

Now, Kat sat in Dr. Murphy's classroom after spending the better part of the weekend in a deep state of complacency. It took everything in her to wake herself up, to crawl towards her disorganized closet and put something on. Her boyfriend, who attended another university five hours away, had recently left her to endure the darkest days alone. He did not know how much she relied on his visits, at each break, or extended weekend, which distracted her from her reality in ways he could never conceive.

"How black is my soul- a mirror of my treacherous thoughts," Kat scribbled onto the notebook paper before her.

It was her final semester as a twenty-seven-year-old single mom who had only attended part-time for years. She sat next to Emma, the brunette with dark and wandering eyes. Emma appeared to have just come out of deep hibernation and was seeing the world for the first time. Already bored with her surroundings, Kat placed her head on her section of the table-like desk and closed her eyes.

VITA

The week before, Vita sat beneath her favorite oak tree in City Park and watched as the Spanish moss swayed in the wind. Despite the weather forecast, she was sure it was going to rain. Predicting the weather was something she had prided herself on; it was something she and her father made a game of when she was just a girl. Sitting on their front porch, he'd say, "I bet you five dollars it's going to rain before daylight ends."

He was always right. This never stopped Vita from opposing him, though, even if she, too, thought it was going to rain. No longer distracted by the Spanish moss, Vita observed her surroundings and focused on the women who walked past her pushing baby strollers. They seemed so happy to console their crying children. Then, there was the woman across the street from the park who struggled with groceries bags, all while the husband walked behind. *My God, that man is standing right there! Never lifting a finger to help her,* she thought before opening her journal.

Vita, particularly excited about the upcoming semester, was interested in education, interested in learning, "very much, in the same way, my friends are interested in giving the most popular guy at their university a blow job," she told her friend Nora once.

"Passionately, willingly, and disturbingly."

Vita did date, however, and she dated a man named Grayson. She found the relationship suffocating at times; she was only 21 and knew at her core, the whole world was at her fingertips if she made the best choices for herself. Outside of the relationship. Grayson, however, wanted to get married after college. *Maybe*, she thought when he let the words fall from his lips, *if he understands that marriage doesn't mean giving away my freedom, my relationship with myself.*

A child ran before Vita, a girl of about six, and a little boy chased her. Of course, the little girl had no idea that someone or something would always be chasing her. Vita gripped her pen tighter. *"Run away, little girl, someday you'll too, be a runaway woman."*

Now, she waited patiently for class to begin. So far only four other students, all women, had arrived. Her eyes fell onto Jo who was wearing an olive-colored shirt.

DE-DE

After being awarded several scholarships, De-De chose to attend the University of New Orleans because it was Louisiana's first and second largest racially integrated university. It meant a lot to her to occupy a space rooted in diversity. Though she didn't know what to expect and had only made assumptions regarding the type of lecturer Dr. Murphy might be, she hoped that she'd be inclusive in her choice of writers to review, capable of speaking about those who write from a diverse perspective.

At the desk, De-De began to fixate on the awkwardness that would take place once her professor would read the N-word out loud from one of their required texts, just like they always did. In that, "It's okay to say it for educational purposes" sort of tone. A moment or two later, Dr. Murphy walked into the room, owning it.

Will this course be a safe space for discourse and intellectual diversity? De-De hoped more than anything that the class would be an intellectual refuge. Just two nights before, she shut herself in the bathroom to avoid any interaction with her roommate and the girl's boyfriend. The two of them had a compulsive need to smoke pot. De-De listened to their PDA while trying to read *The Bluest Eye*. *Forget ever opening a book; all they want to do is open her legs.*

EMMA

Her parents didn't know her, not really. No one knew her. She felt everyone looked at her strangely because she wasn't like the other women they saw around town. No, she was not the same. She sat thinking about her plans for the weekend, and how they were always the same, too.

Read, write, and observe. Read, write, and sometimes she wished she were someone else: anyone else, even a man. *If I were a man, avoiding those questions would be easy.* Emma was only interested in her animals, words, Ruth and God. *My God, why did you make me who I am?*

Ruth and Emma had been friends for years. No one had spoken to Emma in the same way that Ruth did, make eye contact, or receive her with a warm smile. Emma met her at the New Orleans Public Library, and soon it was where they often met to discuss the latest book they had read, or a poem Emma had written. She expressed herself with words, and Ruth expressed herself with sex, but their friendship was an enticing balance. Emma felt she was nothing like Ruth; Ruth was beautiful, round, with a womanly face and body, while Emma had often been described to have "a skinny boy" frame; the head full of hair her mother had forbidden her to cut, her only redeeming quality.

During the summer, she and Ruth met every day at 4:00 p.m., except for Sunday. Ruth knew how important Emma's Sundays were, a time she entirely dedicated to God. However, now that summer was ending, she noticed that Ruth had been too busy to meet up with her—Ruth was dating, and it had become her number one priority. When the two of them were given the time to meet up, most of their conversations revolved around Tom, his penis, and how he had chosen to use it on a particular night.

Ruth would laugh and get red in the face during their discussions, while Emma stared at her in disbelief. She felt that Ruth was so much more authentic when she wasn't dating.

Emma hadn't bothered reaching out, but instead chose to wait because of fear; she feared the complex emotions that the thought of Ruth and Tom's intimacy made her feel, the rage. For reasons like these, Emma often felt it better to remain alone, detached. For the time being, her mind wandered for a bit before she settled on the page she was looking for in the textbook. *I will do some light reading. Stay ahead.*

Rubbing her thumb over the indentations on her index finger, Emma pinched herself for forgetting to take more breaks when writing. "You need to take better care of your hands Emma, they are so rough, like a man," her mother commented once.

Bringing herself back to the present moment, a petite blonde woman who looked as if she had not slept for days came and sat beside her, offering Emma a stranger's smile, the type of smile that is given without revealing teeth. Uncomfortable with most social interaction, Emma who had been homeschooled her entire life, politely nodded in response. *Sometimes it's better to say nothing at all.*

She wasn't there to make friends.

JO

The previous night, Jo's friend danced towards her with a drink in his hand.

"What's the matter with you? It's Pride Night!" he said in all his gay glory.

"Every night is pride night; what do you mean?" Jo asked.

"Exactly!"

Most of her friends happened to be gay men, and unfortunately for her, the places that they frequented never had any gay women. And if they did, it was women with short hair, that sported stud earrings, eyebrow piercings, and work boots; women who felt confident that they should have been born men or felt more comfortable being masc. presenting. *Nothing wrong with it*. Jo had had her share of experiences with more masculine presenting women, but she couldn't deny she was femme for femme and always had been.

"I'm just not feeling it tonight, Gare," she said to him. The truth was that she had just seen her ex-girlfriend, a woman who'd made a point to show up at her doorstep every few weeks after settling for a relationship with a man. Jo had a feeling that she would no doubt show up that night too. The thought of the situation between them left a bad taste in Jo's mouth.

Jo put her cigarette out and swallowed the last of her drink. *This has to be my last cig*. She knew it was time for her to go home. Something had been happening inside of her, her psyche. Jo had lost interest in most of which used to bring her joy. Now, everything, including drinks with her friends, emphasized the wretched emptiness that created an ache in the pit of her stomach.

"I'll see ya later; I gotta go get some sleep," she said to her friend, who was already walking away.

Choosing to ride the 1977 Caliente that she purchased for sixteen dollars at the local Goodwill, Jo smiled when she noticed that it was still locked to the metal bike rack outside of the bar. After learning the hard way, Jo made sure to wrap the chain around more than once. The pink Caliente was her third bike, the first two were stolen on account of her carelessness. She was like her mother always suggested, too trusting. Just like riding her bike home from a bar, most people would not dare attempt to ride a bike home after bar hopping, but Jo knew that a skinned knee and busted lip were better than driving a car and risking her life, or worse, the life of someone else.

She did not have a driver's license, anyway. She never went back to the DMV after she was given a learner's permit. Jo broke the law as soon she sat in the driver's seat without someone above the age of twenty-one sitting beside her. It was her own dirty secret, one that no one knew, not even her own mother.

Jo reached into her backpack to pull out the portable CD player she owned for nearly three years; the black electrical tape she used to wrap around the wires started to become sticky, leaving a residue at the tips of her finger whenever she tried to manipulate it. Out with the CD player came a folded piece of paper, and Jo recognized it to be her class schedule. She stood for a moment, looking at it beneath the old and battered banner that read "Cafe Lafitte."

It read:

1100 French Culture and Civilization 3Cr.

ENGL 2378 Introduction to

Women's Literature-Short Stories and Poetry 3 Cr.

ENGL 3399 Senior Honors Thesis.

ENGL 4161 Advanced Painting 3Cr.

Enrolling in university had given her something to do, time to figure out what she wanted to do with her life—which she now knew was to always create. Jo stuffed the schedule into her back pocket, not caring if it got wrinkled. *Just a few more weeks,* she thought as the pace of her peddling increased. Her smile widened at the thought of the Women's Literature course because it was being taught by Dr. Murphy, and because just like all the literature-related courses she'd taken before, it would give her at least one thing to look forward to.

Jo's desire to study beneath Dr. Murphy first began a year or so prior when she was racing to class and passed by Dr. Murphy. Dr. Murphy was standing before a male colleague at the time, and when she and Jo locked eyes, time stood still. The man kept talking, never acknowledging the professor's need to break away, but Dr. Murphy never let her eyes off of Jo — who, as a result, in a trance-like state, nearly tripped over the first step of the staircase. Jo saw something in Dr. Murphy's eyes that she had only ever seen in her own. After that moment Jo found herself curious about the woman, who she was, and what she taught. It was only after a small amount of research that she had learned that Dr. Murphy was a professor, who was offered a tenured position just two years after her arrival.

Jo was both intimidated and deeply intrigued by her own perception of Dr Murphy, the woman's identity. Now, Jo sat near the back of the classroom, unable to take her eyes off the woman's brown hair, which was thick and hung down past her shoulders. It was strategically pushed away from her face, revealing a round, soft jaw. Dr. Murphy's eyes, two cinnamon-colored flames, captivated Jo.

Her own light brown eyes, which were enhanced by dark shadows that she hadn't bothered to conceal, stared at Dr. Murphy unblinking as she watched her pick up a piece of chalk with her right hand to write on the chalkboard. Her silver bangles clinked together like a wind chime. Jo had to shift in her seat to try and ease the tingling that was beginning to happen between her thighs.

In large cursive letters, Dr. Murphy wrote:

"*Dr. Murphy. Women's Literature,*" before turning towards the five of them and saying:

"You may call me Dr. Murphy. And nothing else. I worked hard for my PhD. I look forward to this semester, the very first semester that I have had the privilege of having an all-female class."

Vita's eyes widened. She looked around at the rest of the students.

"This is it?" she said.

"Yes. This is it!" Dr. Murphy's cinnamon-colored eyes scanned the room expectantly, hopefully, and then fleetingly met the eyes of Jo.

After a brief pause, she continued.

"I will call your name. Please raise your hand if you are in attendance," already knowing that they were. After all, it was a class of only five students.

"Kat Washington." The stringy blonde effortlessly raised her hand. And quite lazy too. The single mother, who according to other professors, had a talent for manipulating words and the skill to describe things, people, and scenarios with ingenuity—when she submitted assignments.

"Vita Jacobs," she, instead of raising her hand, spoke proudly, "In attendance." Dark hair, dark, nearly black eyes, and a particularly strong nose. The one with money.

"Josephine Sallow." Jo raised her hand before Dr. Murphy could finish saying her last name. She had curly hair. An Artist that wrote too. Changed her major three times. Took Women's Gender and Sexuality the previous semester and little did Jo know, Dr. Murphy remembered her well.

"Emily (Emma) Conley." Averted her eyes—the hermit with all A's.

"De-De Abbott." High cheekbones, 4.0 GPA, confident dissenter.

"Here," she said while adjusting the collar of her blouse.

"Ok, we are all here, today, I would like to get to know you; I would like each of you to write a reflection, a reflection on the last bit of literature you've read about a woman or was written by a woman. What did you think of it? Why? We will do this and review the class syllabus."

She then turned to write something else on the board.

What is your favorite color?

Favorite way to pass time?

One place you would like to visit.

Anything I should know about you?"

"Your reflection needs to be at least ten to twenty sentences. There are no rules, no standards; just write. Just for fun, you can answer these questions too. Tell me something about yourself," she said, pointing to the board.

"I also want to say that I expect you all to come to class prepared."

Jo raised her hand, and Dr. Murphy motioned for her to speak.

"Can someone please give me a piece of paper and a pen?" she asked no one specifically, slightly embarrassed.

Jo knew that Dr. Murphy had made the request that the students come to class prepared because of her lack of preparedness. After all, she was the only student to not have at least a notebook on her desk. In fact, the only object that Jo had on her desk was a book, a worn-out copy of *The Alchemist,* one that had been given to her by an acquaintance named Francesca in her early twenties.

Francesca was an Italian woman with volatile mood swings. Her diet consisted of cheese and olives, and she rode a vintage motorcycle. She'd walk around her apartment half-naked, in a pink wig——barking out orders to whichever man she was interested in that month. She was all over the place, and Jo admired her for it. Her wild spirit. To be that careless, to be that free, and still have the whole world eating out of the palm of her hand was a result of the otherworldly beauty she possessed. And a result of Francesca knowing how to use it. Jo too, like all the boys found herself in a trance the moment Francesca confessed to her one night on the small balcony that had become their most coveted hang-out spot: "I've never wanted to kiss a woman before until you."

After Francesca made the confession to Jo, she completely disappeared, only appearing again several months later, out of thin air, to offer Jo the book. Always a woman with a book for Jo.

"You can't keep this book," Francesca said to her.

"You have to pass it along, like someone passed it to me."

"I'm leaving," she continued saying, her yellow-colored eyes bright with passion.

"I'm gonna get out of this town. Read it, you'll see."

Jo never saw Francesca again, and the last thing she had heard was that she'd gotten married and moved to Colorado. Francesca likely felt then exactly what Jo felt, there, at her desk towards the back of Dr. Murphys classroom, a type of emptiness she couldn't yet describe.

"I will," she told Francesca on the day that she left, and Jo hadn't put the book down since. It had become a security blanket and because she had developed such an attachment to the book, she opted to instead *give* the book to herself.

Kat, sensing Jo's embarrassment, quickly reached into her backpack and took out a fresh sheet of paper and one black pen before walking over to Jo's desk. "At least one other person in this class doesn't have their shit together," Kat mumbled to herself.

"Thank you," Jo said and anxiously began to write. They all began to write.

DR. MURPHY

After heating up leftover pasta from the night before, Dr. Murphy tied her hair up in a bun and stuck a red pen deep inside. She poured a glass of merlot and made her way to the dining room table before she began to finger through the five pieces of paper she had placed before her.

Dr. Murphy quickly wrote *"Beautiful"* in bold letters on De-De's paper, then put it in a folder before reaching for the last one.

It was Jo's, and she had written much more than was required of her. Dr. Murphy took a bite of pasta and a long thirsty swallow from the crystal wine glass she used; scanned through two paragraphs about "Everyday Use," by Alice Walker and put a check mark of approval on Jo's paper. After noticing that something had been written on the back, Dr. Murphy flipped the page over to read it too.

"I am a woman who loves women."

Dr. Murphy chewed on the top of her pen and rubbed her neck; it had grown tense from holding her head in the same position for too long. *Her favorite color is yellow,* she thought after continuing to read what was at the top of the page. She then put the piece of notebook paper into the same green folder as the others before stuffing the whole of it into her leather bag.

That night when Dr. Murphy went to bed, she decided to sleep naked. When she slid under her freshly washed linen sheets, the warmth from the dryer made her nipples erect, and she felt a hint of arousal. She desired her husband, and with her hand gliding over her smooth body, she found her wetness.

Her hand rubbed the part that pulsated most intensely as she gave in to its throb. She thought of her husband's heavy, large hands, and of him entering her. Flashes of Jo intercepted intrusively.

"I am a woman who loves women."

And she came. She had come harder than she had in a long time.

One week later, ten glossy eyeballs stared back at Dr. Murphy, their faces illuminated beneath the fluorescent lighting that dulled even the best skin. No matter how many years she taught, Dr. Murphy could never get used to being the center of attention.

The anxiety it caused made her pinch the palms of her hands in search of relief while she took a moment to collect her thoughts. Dr. Murphy could only think of one thing; teach the lesson outside, where she could breathe and release the anxiety, she kept pent up inside.

Once out, Emma let down her hair, pushed two chairs together, and used them as a daybed. Nearing Fall, lying underneath the sun and reading was the exact sort of thing she would do if she were at home, in her backyard. She took out the textbook and flipped to pg.121, *"In the "Fall," at the end of the day, you should smell like dirt."* Emma read.

Emma loved the Fall, and in the Fall, she often smelled like dirt or like the layer of dust on an old book that was long forgotten and shoved away in someone's attic; she typically dug in her family's garden with bare hands. Even if it wasn't producing yield. *Weeds always need pulling.* Closing her eyes, Emma lifted her face towards the sun.

Meanwhile, Kat wondered first about her children and then her boyfriend. *Are they all happy? What are they doing? Glad to be away from me and my unstable moods?*

Kat pictured her children running and playing outside at the daycare. Knowing that she could never provide that sort of happiness to them—Kat pictured the jungle gym, chain-link swings, and clouds that make pictures only children could see. *And him? Is he out and about? Checking out other women as they navigate their way about the university's property in revealing dresses and short shorts?*

Her own mind was getting to her, she hoped that her boyfriend was, as he said, only always thinking of her and the thought of him not made her heart skip a beat.

Kat tied her hair into a tight ponytail and turned to Pg.121 before letting her eyes slide over to where Jo leaned over the edge of the dock that led to the university's lake. *Like a child stuck in a woman's body*, Jo was almost too fascinated with the water or the fact that the day's class would be held outside.

Kat, as an afterthought, wondered about Jo's race, obviously black; *Is she all black? And does it bother her if she isn't? How old is she? What is her degree plan?* These were the sorts of details that Kat wondered about people, the things that set them apart and made them who they were. Things she liked to write about.

Jo—who wasn't racially ambiguous— hadn't had a hard time, even though people did ask her. "You are a Black girl, even if you are mixed," her mother told her one day whilst the two of them looked in a mirror when she was a child. Still, Jo never liked the idea of being put into a box, some economic, social, or racial class. It was the one thing Jo hated most.

Does a person have to perform in a certain way because they are a particular race? Or because they are in a specific social class? She often contemplated. Jo made the decision very early on in her life that she would never let those sorts of things define her, her actions, or her dreams, even if that meant ignoring when they did.

Even if it meant forcing away the recollection of the one time a white customer refused to hand his money to her when she worked as a cashier. She stuck her hand out with a big smile, expecting a courteous exchange, but he quickly sat the money down on the corner of the counter as if he had accidentally touched her, he would have caught some mysterious disease.

The Black Plague. His change was $2.68 cents, and in response to his actions, Jo sat all 0.68 cents of the change down on the counter with his receipt, still holding on to her large courteous, "Fuck you," inspired smile. The man looked at her as if he were offended, and she looked at him back, as if what she did was as natural as what he had just done to her. She watched as he picked up the two quarters, a dime, and eight pennies.

"I am out of nickels," she had said to the man.

The truth was that she felt her identity shouldn't be anyone's concern. But of course, her identity, sexual, political, and racial, was always a concern; she knew this. People were placed in boxes, and their value was measured unfairly without any regard to intersectionality—the complexities of existing in a world where marginalization's overlap.

Dr. Murphy watched as the students, all unique in their potential, navigated around the dock and settled themselves on one of the chairs and benches made available to them. She liked the fact that they were all so supportive of her idea to teach in an unorthodox way. Her dress, which she would have admitted if asked, was a bit too short, and the cool breeze brushed past her legs to remind her. Her pointed ankle boots, which she had owned since her early twenties, did little to protect her ankles and she made a point of finding a seat directly beneath the sun, where she could feel the warmth. Dr. Murphy noticed what the others were wearing; baggy jeans, wrinkled shirts, striped pants, and high-waisted Levi's. She thought the meshing of her students' personalities was exciting and took a moment to observe them before beginning her lecture.

"Kate Chopin, are any of you familiar?" she had asked as she squinted at the pages.

It was then that Jo, for no reason at all, naively sat on the ground across from Dr. Murphy and leaned against the wooden post of the dock, not realizing until she saw the upper part of Dr. Murphy's thigh how it must've appeared to the others. She quickly stood up, embarrassed that she sat on the ground in the first place.

Vita giggled, "Of course we are familiar."

De-De grunted and said, "Yeah, we sure do...It is all they teach about."

"Who are they?" Emma questioned.

"She means white women" Dr. Murphy suggested, "Am I right?"

De-De's mouth formed into a smirk.

Dr. Murphy, being utterly familiar with the lack of African/Black writers presented in most literature classes, understood where De-De came from.

"Yea, I like Kate Chopin, but I like others too. Others like me; no one ever wants to discuss their works; I don't mean to offend you all, but also, if you are offended, I think my people have been offended too, for far too long."

Emma, almost asleep, nodded her head. "Yea, yea, you're right. We never did discuss the works of many African Americans in class. In high school at least, except for stories about slavery, well, at least not in my high school classes. Not like we discuss the classics. It is funny; I never thought about it that way."

"You wouldn't have to," said Kat in reply.

Dr. Murphy, who felt a phenomenal, energetic pull as the nerves in her brain went wild at the unprovoked yet critical discussion that had just manifested. Discourse was, in many ways, one of the better contributions of higher education.

"Jo, what do you think?" Dr. Murphy asked.

"The lack of representation can sometimes go unnoticed because people are so used to not having any. You can't perceive the lack of something you never had. I think that was my experience." Jo looked forward through the group, focusing her attention on the lake before continuing.

"We also must remember that most black authors we *do* learn about stuck to the genre, a specific theme, or narrative that got them the most acclaim. Black American writers were/are either boxed in or excluded altogether. No in between. It's as if civil rights, and the troublesome plight of a black man or woman became the only narrative in publication—as if there were no other narratives for us to fulfill. I get having representation, but at what point are black people going to be represented in a different way? Representation isn't just about seeing someone who looks like yourself. It's about shared experiences too."

"The narrative translates the same time and time again, because the same issues occur, time and time again." De-De mumbled. "And this is America."

Dr. Murphy cleared her throat, "I think that we have a whole semester—- and you all have to trust that I will celebrate the ethnic voices too — even the names of those who many don't speak of. But for now, we will start with "The Awakening." Satisfied with Dr. Murphy's response, each of the students began to focus their attention on the text before them.

Later in the evening, Dr. Murphy, and her husband Bennette spoke on the phone. He asked about her day professing and told her about all the new food he was making and tasting. "Real cultured dishes," he said, "Asados, Mollejas covered in a tangy sauce," he continued, speaking of the sweetness of the Mollejas.

"A very sweet bread, sweet as you," he told her.

Dr. Murphy held onto the phone tightly, trying to taste the flavors, visualize their texture, before she asked about his colleagues.

"How are they? Who are they? Do you like them?"

There was an awkward silence.

"Hello, are we breaking up?" Dr. Murphy added.

"Nope, no, I am here," he said. "Sorry, we are out at dinner right now. I stepped away just after Summer spilled her drink over Robert's plate. "They are all at the dinner table trying to help clean up the mess."

"Summer? Is Robert her husband?" Dr. Murphy asked.

"Oh no, he probably wants to be, but that would never happen," he said, chuckling.

"Well, you never know," she said. "Love happens when people least expect it!"

"Yea, but Summer isn't the type of woman to…" his phone began to crackle again.

"What was that? She isn't the type of woman to what?"

"Honey, I've got to go, I've been away for long enough...the...the connection is bad... love."

And then there was a sudden click.

Dr. Murphy held the phone to her ear a little longer before pressing the end button and sitting it down next to her own early dinner. *Another night of chicken for me*. She eyed the chicken with disgust before suddenly losing her appetite.

So, exactly what type of woman is Summer? She thought as she cleared her dinner plate.

VITA

Vita's brothers were rough housing in their home's lavishly styled foyer while her father went on yet another rant about the fundamentals of being politically intelligent.

"Politics are a gamble," he said, "either way you look at it, in order to make a difference, you really have to understand politics. You must understand the history. Everything that is worth considering must come from considerable history."

Vita scoffed, "What does that even mean?" she asked as she swiped at her brother's head.

"It means, Vita, that if you must study and you must write, you must consider history," he said, taking a drag of his thinly rolled cigar. Vita's mother hated its smell but had no real authority over what her father did. He had habits, and she had long given up on trying to control them.

Vita watched as her father raised his hand to clear the smoke.

"But I am not interested in politics," she said.

"Ahh, but as someone who's in academia and interested in the art of writing, you must always consider the current state of affairs, and the current state of affairs of the world is almost always directed by politics. Understanding political history will simply make you a better author."

There was no way to contradict her father; once he made his mind up, it was cemented in existence forever more.

Vita was grateful that he encouraged her desire to write, to express herself, yet she sensed that he supported her education just to appease her. She knew that he didn't truly value her creative pursuits, or the degree that she would one day acquire, at least not in the way that he valued the potential of her brothers who only focused on having fun. Their path was already laid out for them, to work for their father, marry, and have children. And they were fine with it.

Vita's mother called to her from their kitchen, and she couldn't help but roll her eyes.

Off to the duties of womanhood.

Dr. Murphy had introduced a poem earlier in the week, and as Vita made her way toward her mother, her womanhood, and the kitchen, the words appeared in her mind's eye:

"The door is closed; the chairs, the tables, the steel bowl, me." *

Vita had it down to science really, if she played her mother's game, she could do whatever she pleased and that meant spending more time with Grayson. If all she had to do was wash a few dishes to be free from her mother's gaze, she'd do it. It was already 30 minutes until his planned arrival, and Vita planned to stay out late.

"Did you come yet?" Grayson asked several hours later. Vita couldn't be bothered, in her mind, she was reciting Louisa May Alcott repeatedly.

"Don't drive me away,
But hear what I say:
Bad men want the gold.
They will steal it tonight,
And you must take flight.
So be quiet and busy and bold.
"Slip away with me,
And you will see...."

For the life of her, she couldn't remember the rest of the poem. And it bugged her.

"Yes, a lot." She lied.

Though she had read the Alcott poem several times, on that day, that specific visit with Grayson, she had been reminded of it and she couldn't get it out of her head. Grayson, done and lying on top of her in the backseat of his new Pontiac Bonneville, inhaled and exhaled heavily.

"It's so tight in here, I can barely breathe," she said, trying to get him off of her. His sweat drenched her body, and the perspiration of the event left the windows of his new car fogged.

"This is the very best baby," he said as he lifted himself off her and then wiped her clean with his T-shirt.

"Have you thought about what I asked?" He questioned her.

"Yes, about Thanksgiving break," she said still trying to remember the last lines of the Alcott poem. Grayson looked at her, confused.

"What are you talking about?"

What a wise little thing am I;
For the road, I show
No man can know,
Since it's up in the pathless sky."
Vita blurted out loud.

"That's it!!" she proclaimed; her body reacted almost as dramatically as it would have responded had she orgasmed in the way that Grayson wanted her to.

"What's it?" Grayson, now annoyed, asked.

"The poem, the poem, I was trying to…" she stopped mid-sentence and followed Grayson's eyes as they shifted forward, unwilling to meet hers. He was shutting her out.

"You asked me about Thanksgiving break, my plans, right?" She asked.

"NO, I mean, yes, I did, but that was weeks ago; I am asking about what we talked about last week, about marriage!"

He was now looking directly at her. Marriage, the question. She had tried her very best to pretend as if she had never heard his question in the first place.

"Oh, that question, well, I mean, we haven't even had Fall break yet, Grayson what is the rush?" she replied.

"I mean, honestly… I plan on attending graduate school."

"Rush? To say we would be rushing is to say that we need time to think about it, we don't need more time to think about it. I already know what I want."

Grayson started the ignition of his new car.

"You make it sound like a transaction, a business deal. One that only you benefit from" Vita said, to which Grayson didn't respond.

The two of them drove home in silence, and when they arrived at the end of the driveway to Vita's home she exited the vehicle anxiously, surprised that he didn't walk her to her front door. She wondered after he drove off where the so-called gentlemen he claimed to be had gone.

KAT

Kat waited patiently in the psychologist's office on Friday. She had frequented the office every other Friday for weeks to receive therapy and competent consideration of her medications.

"Kat, you may come back," the secretary declared.

Eagerly, Kat stood up and rushed through the open door that the secretary stood holding.

She was grateful for therapy, the potential that her depression could be cured, that some new medication would help—A futile hope, it seemed.

The psychotherapist sat in a black leather chair. His glasses settled at the tip of his nose. He adjusted them habitually and often. *He has a sort of tic*, Kat thought once, *one with his vocal cords*. At the end of each sentence, he'd make a repetitive noise. An "amh" of some sort, the unnecessary clearing of his throat.

"How are you feeling?" he asked, before making the "Ahm" sound instead of looking up at her.

"Is the new medication working?"

"It isn't working yet," she said, "I hoped that this time it would work."

"Well, it doesn't happen overnight," the man said. Give it more time; this is your second medication in six months."

Always, always more time. Has it been six months? She thought. *I don't have more time. Each day I am closer to giving in.*

It wasn't his fault, though; Kat never disclosed the full details of her everyday life. The fact that she cried every day, cursed at her kids, locked herself in the bathroom as they yelled out to her. He also didn't know that she drank till she vomited sometimes, nor that she had already written the letters goodbye, already decided the way. All he assumed was that she had gotten depressed after the birth of her first child.

Bipolar Depression, Borderline Personality Disorder, what is the diagnosis? The truth is you don't fucking know do you?

"Post Partum," he said when he first began seeing her. Of course, she never told him that she had felt that way since before the birth of her first child, who was conceived under traumatic circumstances. Kat learned that the mention of her children got her further in her quest for support. It seemed to Kat that, no one cared when a woman complained of symptoms until a child or man was involved—when her ability to nurture and care for another became impossible. Then and only then would her health be prioritized.

"What if this medication doesn't work? What are my options?" Kat asked.

"If this medication doesn't work, we could look at other options. All we can do is try to manage it, which is what we are trying to accomplish by these visits," the psychotherapist said while writing new notes to put into Kats' file.

Oh, I manage it, manage it with alcohol, writing, and not being alone.

"Well, yes, and for that, I am always grateful," Kat said instead of what she was actually thinking.

She looked forward to going home and drinking, shutting the door, and keeping the world from realizing the truth. Wanting to cry, she laughed instead, imagining her lipstick leaving a stain at the edge of a wine glass, or beer bottle. A smiling crescent moon. The vividly evident truth is that the darkness was winning, the truth that her boyfriend was her only redeeming distraction to a life she felt she had been forced into because of guilt. Either way, for Kat, if she wanted to manage her mental health, everything needed to fall in place so that she could spend time with him, balancing love, motherhood, and college.

Often instead of attending class, she prepared for her boyfriend's visit by cutting out recipes and going grocery shopping. She did the piles of laundry that had been building up in her small apartment and drove to a liquor store to buy vodka and sparkling wine.

When Kat and her boyfriend made plans her mood shifted; she was no longer a poor single mom but a single mom with a man. Her man, a dark brunette with a five-o'clock shadow, was 6ft4, and naturally muscular. When he visited, they would stay up late, often into the early morning reading what she had written. He would try his best to follow along, and Kat appreciated his attempts to understand what she was writing about.

"Read me one of your poems," he'd say to her after their most intimate moments, and she would.

After Kat left her therapy session, she waited for her boyfriend's arrival while re-reading a specific poem from the chapter Dr. Murphy assigned for homework. At 8:50pm, twenty minutes past the time he was to arrive, she began to pace.

Kat walked around her dining room table and looked out the window whenever a car would drive by; their headlights beamed through her slightly open blinds. She experienced a roller coaster of emotions; excitement, sadness, and frustration all at once. *He should be here already! This isn't like him*, she thought before the phone rang, breaking the silence.

"Hey, baby," he said as if he had not left her waiting. As if her mental stability did not depend on his arrival.

"Hi," she said, glancing through the blinds once more. The cord of the phone wrapped around her wrist several times over.

"Are you almost here?" She said, half hopeful, half knowing that he was calling to cancel. Woman's intuition.

"I forgot about my friend's party and already committed to going; I got the dates mixed up, babe," he said to her, speaking to her as if she were a child.

Kat grabbed a handful of her hair and pulled until she heard a few strands snap. Fighting back tears, she bit down on her bottom lip to allow the skin to split in the same spot it always had, right at the center. Her tantrums were ritualistic.

"So, you're not coming?" she asked, wrapping her blonde hair around her fingers—another habit she had picked up as a girl.

"Probably not this weekend, forgive me?"

"It's fine," she said coldly and disconnected the line.

When he called her back, not once, but twice she ignored the ringing. By his second attempt, she was already reaching for the brand-new vodka she had stashed in the cupboard above the stove. Kat hadn't eaten anything because she had been waiting for him, for the two of them to enjoy the dinner she made together, and now her dinner would become a tumbler full of vodka, poured to the rim, which she would chug like water.

"That bitter sin," her mother used to call it.

What good is food if you have no one to enjoy it with, she thought, and drank.

Stumbling, Kat made her way toward her bedroom, where her two children slept innocently. Climbing between them in the bed they had claimed as their own, she felt grateful that she at least had their warm bodies to lie next to, two tiny humans full of love.

The following day Kat had a radiating headache. Her two children, who would wait for no one, had already rummaged through the refrigerator, and a collection of opened and unopened things lay in a discombobulated pile before the television.

"My sweet baby girl," she said, rubbing her fingers through her daughter's hair.

Her son asked for eggs.

"Eggs, ok, sure," she told him and made her way to the cupboard above the stove, the one she visited the night before, and took one swig of vodka. Her children studied her with inquisitive eyes as she held the bottle to her lips.

EMMA

"How are things with Tom?" Emma said, choosing to bring up a subject she knew Ruth would be most interested in.

"Tom, ha, he uses his mouth in more ways than I can count."

Ruth was flipping through the pages of a gossip magazine and Emma could hear it through the phone each time she turned one of the pages.

"It says here," Ruth said, "Men don't want a woman that is easy to get, and they need a challenge."

"Well, isn't that how you got Tom? "Emma said,

"No, I don't think so," Ruth responded, still flipping through the pages, "I think I was pretty forward with him."

"He is on his way now."

Ruth continued after having already put the magazine down to pluck her eyebrows. Emma and Ruth had been on the phone for over an hour and Emma knew that mentioning Tom's visit was Ruth's way of politely excusing herself from the conversation.

Emma could picture Ruth looking in the mirror, perfecting her hair, and spraying perfume just minutes before Tom would knock on her door. She imagined the way Tom would touch her. The flushing of Ruth's cheeks. Emma again grew jealous.

"I'll talk to you later," she told Ruth, who she was sure was only halfway listening anyways.

"Sounds good," Ruth said, before she quickly disconnected the line, leaving no time for Emma to respond.

This upset Emma. Why was it so easy for Ruth to redirect her focus? She knew she herself would be waiting patiently for Ruth's next call, but would Ruth be doing the same? Would she be the first to reach out?

Sitting down now at the edge of her bed, Emma felt a yearning. She wanted to feel what they felt, too, pleasure Emma eyeballed the Russian doll, a gift that her Great Aunt had given her two years prior. She considered how the rounded, smooth surface of it would feel against her, and without giving it much consideration, got up to lock her bedroom door.

Emma removed the throw pillows from her bed and pulled the covers back. After unzipping her skirt, she let it fall to the floor before climbing into the bed with the Russian doll. Images of Ruth and Tom, the two of them together, their naked bodies smashed up against one another; the sweat between them flooded her mind. Feeling increasingly aroused, the Russian doll made her feel the way that she had imagined Ruth did when Tom was inside of her until the only person, she imagined was Ruth. How she smelled, her breast; she couldn't stop herself if she wanted to.

DE-DE

De-De walked slowly through The French Quarter, the oldest neighborhood in New Orleans, or what she liked to call it, The Crescent City. Built on the sharp edges of the Mississippi, it made the shape of a crescent moon, and De-De felt the name was fitting for more than one reason.

De-De watched as a carriage led by a white man and his horse carried around two tourists. *They must be tourists; tourists are the only ones that get excited by such a thing. Tourists all have the same look in their eyes*, she thought as the man whistled while his customers smiled at one another with eager eyes, wanting to swallow the whole of New Orleans in one night. It had occurred to her that people who were born or had lived in New Orleans for a long time, like herself, knew that the real magic was in coffee shops, libraries, and dive bars. Midnight walks around neighborhoods as colorful as the rainbow, musty bookshops, and the Jackson Square regulars——The kids who played their instruments as if their life depended on it. *Maybe their life does depend on it.*

De-De, finally inside of Cafe Du Monde, a coffee shop that she frequented more than any other, placed an order.

"Just one black coffee, please," she said to the cashier, a woman about fifty years old.

"Coming right up; you sure you don't want no creamer?" she said.

"No, thank you." said De-De

"I like to dip my beignet in it; I know it's weird."

The cashier looked at her with surprise; of course, she did; dipping a pastry into black coffee was another habit De-De picked up from her grandmother. She swore sometimes that the woman was an even more significant influence on her life than her own mother.

"Here you go."

De-De took her black coffee and sat by the window furthest away from the entrance of the coffee shop. It was the same spot she always sat, and she brought everything she needed to stay for an extended period, including snacks. It was where she did most of her studying to get away from her roommate.

A moment or so later, a young man with a broad smile and white teeth came up to her, offering her a fist bump.

"My sister," he said.

De-De smiled back; she had been friends with Christopher for a long time, one of the few people she thought she could both have fun with and have an in-depth conversation with. Conversations related to politics, inclusivity, and social constructs.

"How's your women's lit class? Ya gettin' into it?" Christopher asked, genuinely interested in her response.

De-De, already having taken a bite out of her pastry, quickly chewed.

"It's…." she said, unable to finish her sentence.

Quickly losing interest in the need to rush, De-De chose to enjoy the flavor, the stark contrast between the sweetness and smooth texture of the powdered sugar— and the bitterness of the Columbian brew.

She gave Christopher a thumbs up instead. Christopher laughed.

"Good," he said, "Real good" after taking out his textbook and highlighters. De-De, after finishing the very last bite of her pastry, did the same. The two of them were both preparing for their final and very heavily weighted research paper.

JO

I'll take you, you and you. Jo thought to herself, while grabbing the acrylic paints, canvas, and sketch pencils. With it all piled before her on the living room floor, the same spot where she completed all of her creative projects, she painted. Cool tones of blue, and green, smoothed across the canvas depicting the waves of the ocean—-warm tones, a stark contrast to paint the curves of a woman who was immersing her naked body into the sea whilst the sunrise swallowed her whole; Jo portrayed its warmth using the same technique as Georgia O'Keeffe. The colors coral and pink strategically gave the illusion of being up close, close in the same way that a camera lens could be.

Two newspaper articles, one art showing, and one auctioned off art piece, Jo had long given up on her desire to be recognized as a painter even though being glorified in a city like New Orleans was every artist's dream. Jo realized that she valued the act of painting more than the idea of being seen or known as a painter. The work it took to promote herself, too much. In fact, Jo had taken that stance on nearly everything now, including her writing. She hardly ever showed anyone her work anymore and was just beginning to read her writing out loud in Dr. Murphys class.

Jo propped the painting up on the ledge of the window before removing her clothes in preparation for a shower, it was time to get ready for the day.

Tracy Chapman blared in her ears as she rode through Marigny past jazz players, the swooning tourists that dropped change in their buckets and her favorite poster of Stormé DeLaVerie—a phantom of a lesbian woman she'd heard lots about but never actually saw. "Her story lives from NOLA to Europe and New York City," her friend Totty told her during a night of bar hopping.

Jo was on the way to her favorite bookstore, for she loved everything about the place, the smell, and the raggedy staircase that allowed her and others to take advantage of two stories worth of books. Even the little old lady named Dahlia, who always had red lipstick smudged on her two front teeth. "Dahlia on Decatur" or "Decatur Dahlia" is how Jo would refer to the woman when trying to describe her as she wrote in her journal, *"Dahlia on Decatur encouraged me to get this book,"* and *"Dahlia on Decatur told me about the time she rode a horse down Magazine in a Bikini."*

"Sunshine," a black cat, well overweight, made his way between her legs once Jo made it inside. Sunshine made a point of brushing against any visitor that gave him a good ear scratch and Jo made a point to scratch behind his ears each time. Dahlia on Decatur sat on a stool while straightening the new inventory and complaining under her breath. She only stopped what she was doing to say hello to Jo.

"There she is! I was wondering when you were gon turn up again," she said, with that same lipstick-stained smile. Jo never had the heart to tell her, not that she thought Dahlia on Decatur cared either way. The woman was a force to be reckoned with, and likely gave up on trying to avoid the smearing a long time ago.

"Anything good?"

"You mean that lesbian stuff you are always reading about?" Dahlia asked.

"You know it."

Dahlia stood up, approached the small space behind the counter and reached into an almost overflowing cardboard box.

The book that she pulled out was Stone Butch Blues, by an author named Leslie Feinberg, and it was published in 1993.

"Thanks for thinking of me," Jo said, reaching out for the book and then stuffing it into her paper carrier tote. It had become a thing for Jo, she collected lesbian anthologies and books of poetry that were erotic in context and focused on the intimate relationships between women. Dahlia had grown Jo's collection significantly out of the kindness of her heart, only reinforcing her obsession.

Jo allowed herself to get snug in the bookstores most atrocious chair. The chair, after many years of abuse, was permanently impressed– "a testament of all the asses that have sat there before"— Dahlia told Jo when they first met. The thought of Dahlia's statement made Jo giggle while she wrote on the underside of the journal's cover.

"Coriander
Some call it Chinese parsley
The slick texture of a sauteed mushroom
Onions, tomatoes, marinated in lemon juice.
Cocoa,
Pure cocoa, eat.
A sprinkle of sesame seeds
Sweet milk, against the inner flesh of her cheek, she drinks.
Tasting your history
Your hopes
Your aspirations
Your name tag reads DESTINY.
Your lovers look up at you in the back of a dingy kitchen in Chinatown------
They look up as if you are a palm reader, and you open them wide so you can tell them their Fortune.
Closing their eyes, they ignore that you are just another woman from Jersey.
Another sous Chef
Another bowl of orange chicken
Another order of tonight's special, sweet and sour
Another cheap customer who won't tip-------or donate to the deaf and blind kids, whose faces are plastered on glass jars, with scarred and half-open eyelids."

Jo, never having been to China Town in New York City, enjoyed imagining what it would be like. It was easy for her to imagine what it would be like to walk its busy streets just before meeting a masc. lesbian who had a fleet of lovers and a talent for creating fancy cuisine.

Coriander... some call it Chinese parsley.

To the left of her, a bird outside of the window picked up a small twig between its beak and flew above to the height of the window where Jo could no longer see it. Still watching, Jo found herself delighted to see a tiny gray and white feather float down onto the window ledge. She looped her necklace around her index finger, one her mother had given to her on her thirteenth birthday.

"It was your grandmother's mother; I always knew I'd give it to you."

"You mean my great grandmothers?" Jo asked.

"Yes."

The necklace was solid gold, with an angel wing charm. The word Uriel engraved on its back.

"What does Uriel mean?" She asked her mother, struggling to pronounce the word.

"Uriel is the name of an angel; your grandmother's mother was Catholic, and she talked about angels often!"

"Catholic?"

"Yes."

"The word Angel comes from the word Angelos, or Hebrew "Mal' akh" and it means messenger," her mother said, surprising her.

"How do you know that, Mom?" Jo asked her.

"That's what my mother said when she gave it to me. I don't know if it's true, but maybe there's something to it."

Jo didn't ask any more questions, but she did wear the necklace every day and had not taken it off since, not even in the shower. Her grandmother died years before she was born, and the chain made her feel like she had some part of her past because all she had ever known growing up was her father and mother.

It wasn't until Dahlia walked over and nudged her shoulder that she came out of the daze she had been in whilst staring out the window. "Wake up" she teased.

"You know, old lady, it's okay to sit down sometime," she told Dahlia.

"Well, when you have more time behind you than you do in front of you, you start to think about things differently, Jo. I'll get plenty of time to sit or lie down when I'm dead."

"Hm, can't say I've heard that one before!" said Jo.

"Is that why you're always sitting?" Dahlia had jokes.

"No, I'm sitting and thinking…"

Dahlia was now looking out the window too. Her cloudy gray eyes were focused on something out in the distance for a time before Jo realized that Dhalia was actually looking into her own mind, into her own memories, not out the window. The two of them both looked in silence until the ringing of a bell, which meant that a customer walked in.

"See, there's no time to sit down," Dhalia said before patting Jo on the back. Jo stood up, reflecting on what Dhalia said.

More years behind.

Jo always struggled with the idea of time, how people had to trade time for food, a place to stay, and stability. *Time is our most valuable commodity.*

"Dahlia?" Jo asked to which Dahlia responded by turning back to her.

"Do you have any regrets? I mean, you seem to keep busy and tell me all of those wild stories."

"Ha. Regrets?" Dhalia said. "I have very few regrets. Life is too short for regrets Jo, and what's even more important to know is that the world keeps spinning regardless of if you're in it or not."

"What's one?"

"One what?" Dahlia said, a little annoyed.

"Regret? Or story?"

Dhalia took a deep breath.

"My biggest regret, just right off the top of my head, is not knowing sooner that if you don't ask, the answer is always no, and if you don't try, then everything will seem impossible. There were a few times I bit my tongue, and a few opportunities I didn't take. Sometimes, very rarely though, I think about a different life now that I am closer to death."

"What kind of life?" asked Jo.

"Well, now you're just being nosy," Dahlia teased.

"The truth is life is a story, and we all have to be willing to endure the highs and lows of it, including its boring parts. The painful parts. We have to also accept that sometimes a story, our story, won't end the way we hoped it would."

Dahlia, aware of the sheer sadness in Jo's eyes, said, "I hope your story ends the way you want it to though, you got your head on right." Dahlia turned from Jo and made her way to the customer, a woman with curly hair and a nose ring. Looping her finger around her necklace once more, Jo watched as Dhalia wobbled away. *How does she manage to find happiness all alone in this city? How do I manage it?*

Dahlia's, Jo observed, connections came mostly from the characters in the books that she shelved and the customers who bought them. Jo imagined herself as a single old lady, wobbling around an almost empty bookstore, and it was easy to do because she too had been alone her whole life, despite having parents.

Being alone was a character trait that she accepted in the same way a person might accept that they are funny or determined——learning early on that she'd have to experience both the worst and best aspects of her life without the type of companionship most people consider to be detrimental. Being alone was comforting and safe, until it wasn't. Jo stood up and gathered her belongings—What she needed more than anything was to feel a sense of belonging, purpose, and the only place she found it was in the women's literature class.

"Won't end the way we hoped." Jo knew how she wanted her story to end, but knew what Dhalia told her was true, too.

DR. MURPHY

Her face was bare, forty years old. Fine wrinkles appeared where they had never appeared before. More prominently around her mouth, though, for she had spent most of her life offering everyone, even strangers, a smile. She offered a smile even when she was most uncomfortable. It took years of practice to be able to perform that well, too, in various aspects of her life. Like within her marriage, with students, colleagues—and social environments alike. Time and time again her performative disposition, too, gave her good end-of-year student reviews and professional advancements.

Too many festivals, not enough sunscreen, she thought, as she rubbed retinol cream on her face. She wouldn't change it, not really. Her face, or her experiences. Her younger years were spent traveling, roaming the streets of places she had only heard the name of only a week before; her pursuit of knowledge always leading her through a new door.

Those experiences, every choice, her most current beliefs about life, too, were packed tightly together on the shelves of her floor-to-ceiling bookcase. It took nothing more than a quick glance at her bookcase to remind her of where she had been and where she might be going. Stones, ornate frames with tiny pictures in them, concert tickets, Dr. Murphy had created a shrine.

After Dr. Murphy applied her makeup, a deep beige foundation, brown eyeshadow, and mascara, she slipped on a blue dress that she had picked out the evening before. Its polyester material clung to her body as she fastened the tiny button that rested just beneath the nape of her neck.

"There," she said out loud, as if one simple, nice-fitting blue dress was enough to fix the problems of the world and the problems in her life, too.

After arriving at class, Dr. Murphy cleared out her bag. She had previously prepared a lesson that reflected on the life and work of Shirley Jackson. She and her students had already read "The Lottery" and were going to focus on the short story "Flower Garden" before ending the unit. The students exceeded her expectations, and thoroughly moved quickly through the final assignments of the unit. Making annotations and summarizing "The Flower Garden" quickly they still had at least 20 mins left of class.

"Let's gather in a circle," Dr. Murphy suggested. It had become routine for the students to share their work—often. Eager to hear classmates' opinions, Dr. Murphy's classroom was a safe space for them to celebrate creativity.

Dr. Murphy took the seat that Kat would have sat in had she attended class, which was at the desk directly across from Jo. The students flipped through the pages of their journals and notebooks, and Dr. Murphy' felt compelled to focus on the curve of Jo's brows, the plumpness of her lips, and the slender make of her fingers. Just when she glanced beneath Jo's neck, Jo looked up which left her no choice but to quickly avert her eyes. This sent a chill down Jo's spine. She caught her. *She's studying me.* Jo thought. Pretending not to notice the fleeting, alluring, and unexpected gaze of Dr. Murphy, her "straight" professor. She kept her eyes on the textbook and Dr. Murphy shifted in her seat, applying pressure in a way that felt good to her.

"Ok, tell me, what do you guys have? Raise your hand if you want to read something you have written." Only two of them raised their hands.

"Ok, let's start with Vita," she said.

"This is just something I have been working on; I am still working on it, though I work tirelessly at its completion." Usually confident, this time she spoke like a small child, fearing punishment, but read anyway:

"We lay next to each other, with our bare backs against the earth.

But We don't look.

At the brow that is furrowed with curiosity

The eyes, like glass

Brown, evergreen hint
Hair, dark."

Vita, biting her bottom lip, felt the urge to pull out her pen to revise the verse right there in front of them. It took a moment for her to relieve herself of the urge and look at Dr. Murphy, signaling that she had finished her recitation.

"When will you complete it?" Emma asked when Vita stopped reading.

"Oh, I don't know, just playing around really", Vita said, smiling.

De-De implied that she wanted to share her work too, and Dr. Murphy nodded in response, noticing for her to begin.

"This is a journal entry; I wrote it after reading "How It Feels To be a Colored Me," a short story I read in High School; it's a kind of juxtaposition, we all know what Zora Neale Hurston's theme is.

De-De said. "I just wanted to write a poem portraying the mind of another girl—one that might not have had the confidence and audacity that matches Zora's main character in the short story."

"I'm just
A Black, Black, Black night
But I want to be white, white, white.
So that they can see me
Bright, Bright, Bright
 light
I'm just a tiny speck, a tiny grain of sand.
Barely there, in the palm of their hand,
Waiting for the sun to shine
So, I can glisten, glisten, glisten.
Listen
I am just a Black.
Black eye
Black shadow.
Black as midnight
With Black, Black, Black cries

And no amount of shine, no amount of scrubbing
Can erase this bleak Blackness that resides inside."

"Wow, that's amazing, I see what you did there. Have you finished it?" Dr. Murphy asked.

"Well, no, I am still editing it," De-De replied, tapping her pen.

"De-De, your perspective is always so fresh, and I value it," said Dr. Murphy, and after a moment of pause, she continued speaking.

"Anyone else?" She asked, hoping they had more.

No one raised their hand.

"Emma, what about you? Do you have something you want to share?" said Vita, and this made Emma nervous. She looked around at their smiling, blushed faces, and decided she would rather not.

"Nah, I don't have anything I want to share," she said while gathering her belongings, thinking of everything she had been doing—lustful, ungodly things with her Russian doll.

"Ok, that is fine," Dr. Murphy said.

"Do any of you have contact with Kat? She has missed quite a few classes, and I want to be sure she is doing okay."

De-De spoke first. "I don't really know her, but I know where she lives, a person I know has dropped things off for her in the past."

It was a pot that her roommate's boyfriend had dropped off at least once. She recalled. "I could go and check on her."

"Yes, please," Dr. Murphy said, as she wrote her number down on a sheet of notebook paper, "and give this to her. Let her know to call me if she has any questions or needs to talk."

Jo watched as she wrote the number down and quickly memorized it, a skill she learned in grade school by memorizing multiplications, knowing she'd never dare dial it.

"I wrote, I wrote poetry," Jo said, and Dr. Murphy was interested.

"What did you write? Would you like to share?" She asked.

Jo nodded yes, as she pulled out a very worn notebook from her backpack and she read:

"Pretty Things"

"I collect pretty things.
A warm smile, a pair of painted lips
Teeth
Tongue
Cheek
Glossy eyeballs that glisten in the sun
A laugh, thought, or tear.
A lock of hair to braid, to bend at my will.
The mole nearest to the clavicle of a neck
The flare of nostrils, the nook of a philtrum
The plumpness of the breast"

Dr. Murphy sat at the desk completely and unexpectedly aroused, and she watched as Jo's mouth formed a crooked smile. Jo had them hooked like a fish. Never looking up, Jo placed her hand on her neck, and continued:

"Then there are fingers and palms too.
I collect pretty things—Like a pair of legs.
That open, wide
Or Moments filled with love, hate, or fear.
Frozen in time, all of these pretty things
They exist, Here, within my mind's eye."

Everyone snapped their fingers, a milder version of applause, everyone except Dr. Murphy who was trying her best not to look discomforted.

"It's about people watching, or even intimacy, how in those most intimate moments we can sometimes take a picture with our minds. We collect all the unique aspects of a person." Jo spoke, "Time doesn't necessarily erase those things."

"I like it!" said De-De, intrigued. "It's like even after a relationship ends or you see a person for the last time, a piece of them remains, an image, that one small detail that lingers in the back of your mind."

"Yea, I get it too," said Vita, thinking of Grayson.

Dr. Murphy, eager for class to end, stacked the day's books up onto the desk.

"I trust I will see you all bright and early Tuesday morning," she said, "Please bring a paper and pen; we will be writing; writing about what we have read so far in class."

After Dr. Murphy gave the students permission to dismiss, everyone besides Jo hurriedly gathered their belongings and walked out. Leaving Jo to tread just a few steps behind. Dr. Murphy, hoped to God that Jo wouldn't turn around. She didn't.

It was night-time when Dr. Murphy made it home and called her husband. She dialed his number; it rang only two times before she finally got an answer.

"Hellllllllllllllllllllllllllllllo," a woman said.

"Yes, this is Bennette's wife?"

"Bennette, your wife is on the phone," the woman said, not directly answering her.

"Dr. Murphy, I have heard so much about you."

Sounding out the vowels in the word "You" as much as she could.

"Bennette tells me about what you are discussing in your classes, and I only wish I could have taken your class at least once."

Dr. Murphy heard a ruffling of static before Bennette intercepted.

"Hi honey, how are you? So glad you called!"

"Are you?" she asked, jealously.

"Yes! Silly. What are you doing?" he asked, and then, "Summer is here with me now going over the menu, boring stuff but needed," he said as if there was nothing strange about a woman answering his phone.

"I am grading papers. I was hoping to speak to you, but it seems you are busy.... with ...Summer, is it?"

"Yes, that's it…" he said, "Look, can I call you when we are done? Give me thirty minutes?"

"Sure," Dr. Murphy said and hung up.

Still mulling over her and her husband's interaction, thirty minutes passed by, and he had not called back. Feeling disappointed, Dr. Murphy ran herself a hot bath, poured herself a glass of wine, and took one valium. A medication she was prescribed in her early twenties–and now only used at night to avoid the insomnia that her anxiety sometimes caused.

Dr. Murphy began to think of the time Bennette and his sous chef, a long-haired blonde woman was caught fucking on his restaurant's cutting table. On the night that she found them sweaty and intense with their lust, she stood for over five minutes, deciding what to do.

Should I yell out and cause a scene? She thought, *slowly make an exit and pretend to have never witnessed anything at all?* Eventually, Dr. Murphy chose to slowly walk away, never taking any action.

She considered it to be her fault; he was bored. When Bennette made it home, the night of his affair, he quickly professed that he was exhausted and rushed into the shower. Dr. Murphy said nothing. How could she? Not really, not when she had had an equally intense moment a few months before with the woman she had been casually chatting with at the university's library.

Dr. Murphy wondered about Summer, was she dark-haired? Large-breasted? Small? Was she as sexually alluring as the last woman? *Who knows how many women he's cheated on me with*, she thought, knowing that she herself had only stepped out once.

She shifted her focus to the woman she'd slept with, the one who made sure that students were headed in the right direction during their research projects, by helping them gather the most useful resources. Dr. Murphy pictured the woman's preppy attire and thought of her tenacious need to make sure that every book was in its proper place.

It was the woman's structure and organization during such a chaotic time that attracted me to her, NOT the fact that she was a woman, she thought and began to bathe.

VITA

Vita and Grayson walked the length of her family's very large walk-around porch. Her family was hosting a party. "A celebration of life," her mother had said. It was her father's birthday. Most of their guests had already left, and inside the house, there remained just family. Family who had spent most of the evening asking her, "What are your plans after graduation?" or "When will you have children?" And "Why hasn't that handsome man of yours proposed?"

She felt exhausted, the energy that it took to dodge answering them directly was overwhelming, and now Grayson stared off into the yard and avoided her eyes. He sat there stoically sipping his brandy, and that is when she decided that she would start a conversation.

"I have been writing." She spoke.

"Hm," Was Grayson's only response.

"Yea." she paused, unsure whether she should continue. "I have been writing a lot, especially since my professor lets us read some of our work out loud. It kind of motivates me, you know?" She continued.

"Sounds cool," Grayson said, stirring his drink with a thick index finger. Vita hid her disgust, thinking of the germs that likely were beneath his nails.

"Would you like to hear some of it?" she asked, to which he did not reply.

This prompted her to grab her journal, the one with a gold ribbon that she always carried with her. After opening it, she started to read from her most recent entry:

"I can almost hear it, the silence.
Almost see it, an empty room
You can almost taste it, the tangy spice of resentment.

The audacity of me
The coming and going."

Grayson grunted, and Vita continued after clearing her throat:

"And then being afraid to leave.
Nails bit down to blood, but the skin intact.
Picking with teeth at what might have been.
Had I mustered up the courage to step back from that
loaded gun..
I might've been.
But even an old shell of myself."

He grunted again. Vita, in response, kept reading, enunciating every vowel.

"It's something. It's something to those who want me
high on their polished mantle.
cleaned, and then sewn shut.
Stuffed
Antler's protruding
Eyes, black, with a synthetic shine
"This here, this here's my prize."
Poaching me, quit the obsession.
Most prized possession
Poaching me...."

Before she could finish her sentence, Grayson swallowed the rest of the brandy in his glass and blurted out to her, "Alright, so you're a writer; you want us to all sit around and give you praise because, what? Do you know how hard it is to get published? Do you really think this will result in anything?"

Vita grew red in the face, shocked at his rage but even more so at his audacity to not take her seriously as a creative. It was all she could do but scream back.

"Are you fucking serious? What else should I do? Spend my time with you? Follow you around like some puppy—Oh, wait, this is about getting engaged right? I am sick of trying to make you happy, Grayson, what more can you want? I am here, right here, sitting next to you!"

Vita stood up.

"At least I have found something that no one can take away from me, words, intellect, and that includes you! So, what if I don't get published?"

Grayson, surprised at her rage, stood up too. "I hope you find your happiness, Vita, but I can't do this anymore. You treat me like an option, you just use me, you use me for sex and then go write in that little book. "

Her father, after hearing the yells, walked onto the porch.

"What is going on here?" he asked, concerned.

"Why don't you ask her!" Grayson shouted before storming off the porch and starting the ignition of the vehicle he and Vita had just recently had sex in.

Driving off, the tires left behind a cloud of dust and misplaced gravel. Vita stood before her father, who didn't know what to make of it all. "What happened, Vita?" He asked sympathetically, more sympathetic than usual. "Nothing," she said coldly, "I just read. I just fucking read."

DE-DE

De-De, in exceptionally large parachute pants, a crop top, and earrings that hung freely from her ears, knocked on the door, 701 B. No one answered, but she could tell that someone was there because she heard noises, like the noises that one might have heard in a playground.

She knocked again.

"Come on, white girl, don't make me stand here all day; I am trying to be nice. Got me out here knocking like I'm the police," she said beneath her breath.

A few moments later, a stringy blonde-haired little girl opened the door; she couldn't have been more than two. She had markings all over her body, like a pack of markers had exploded onto her tiny frame.

"Mama?" the little girl said. "Hi," said De-De.

"Mama, mamma, mamma," the little girl repeated, nodding her little head.

"Where is momma? Can you go get her?" The little girl only stood in silence.

De-De took a deep breath and pushed the door open wide. She was shocked to see an apartment a complete mess. Dishes, food, trash, and textbooks were all flung carelessly around. Then her eyes met the icy blue eyes of a little boy, a little older than the girl.

"Hi, sweetie, where's your mommy?"

The little boy calmly pointed to a bedroom and then turned his head back to sesame street, Hillary Clinton was guest-starring.

De-De tiptoed towards the bedroom; the door to it was closed after hearing footsteps. She turned to find the little girl following behind her and crouched down to her level. "Hey, hey, shh, shhh," she put her finger to her lips before whispering, "Go and watch TV with your brother; I am just gonna check on Mama, ok?"

The little girl, a scrawny mute, shook her head yes, and walked towards the living room. De-De stood up and took a deep breath and turned to the shut door. She pushed it open. The room was completely bare and organized compared to the rest of the apartment. There existed in it only a nightstand and a mattress that lie directly on the apartment's wooden floor. There in the middle of the bed was a large lump, a lump that she knew could only be Kat.

It was the afternoon, and De-De couldn't think of any reason that Kat would be in bed at that time, with that mess, and two children that she never even knew Kat had, running around. De-De made her way over to the bed and pulled the large comforter back, already expecting to see a sleeping Kat. *Is she sleeping?* De-De thought, her heart beating fast. Kat was not moving at all.

She put her hands beneath Kat's nose and barely felt a breath. *Or maybe she isn't breathing at all.* De-De panicked. *Oh, no, this white girl is dead, and here I am her apartment with these two kids.*

She pushed Kat's lifeless body, but nothing. She pushed again and again and spent the next few minutes shaking her. Just as she was about to run out of the apartment screaming, Kat gasped. Eyes still unopened. Kat rolled over and began to vomit. Violently. De-De watched as a yellow fluid went pouring out, bile, and watched in fear as Kat coughed, as if something were caught in her throat.

"What the fuck? What the fuck are you doing?"

De-De screamed, now both angry and confused. Anger because it was the first emotion she felt when she didn't want to feel anything else, like panic or fear.

Kat, still barely moving, kept hurling.

De-De rushed into the restroom and grabbed a towel, let it run under the rushing sink water and quickly went back to the room where Kat had eventually turned over onto her back.

Kat, panting, said, "Oh my God, where are my children?"

"They are fine," De-De said while wiping the vomit from Kats mouth and hair.

"What are you doing, woman? Your kids are out there all alone, and I don't know anything about kids, but I know that is not good."

"I just can't anymore, I just can't"...Kat repeated those words over and over again, chant-like.

"Can't what, because it doesn't seem like you have a choice" De-De, took a seat next to Kats' stiff body,

"Do I need to call an ambulance?" she asked her but didn't get a response. She looked down to find that Kat was already dozing off again. Several hours later, around 7:30 pm, Kat woke up again, but this time to dry and cracked lips.

"Alex, George!" she called out, with a sheer look of panic on her face. "I am here, I am right here, they are fine; what do you need?"

De-De, never having been in that sort of situation, was surprisingly calm. She never left Kat's side, not really, except to cook for the two children who mostly kept themselves busy with the television.

"Water?" said Kat,

De-De went to the kitchen and poured water into a mason jar that she had filled with ice cubes. She had already put Kat's children to bed, taking out spare blankets from the hallway closet; she made them the best palette she could and read to them a book titled "The Giving Tree."

When she reentered the bedroom, she found Kat sitting up against a stack of pillows, staring at the wall. It was eerie. De-De sat the jar of water next to the bed on the worn nightstand, and Kat grabbed it. She drank from it as if it was the last glass of water she would ever consume.

"I'm dehydrated," she said, and then, "What are you doing here?" Before finishing the last of it.

"Dr. Murphy wanted me to come to check on you; you have been skipping class, and when I came, your daughter." "Here", she reached into her pocket, "she wrote her number down...."

"Alex?" asked Kat, quickly interrupting her.

"Yes, well, Alex, she answered the door naked and just let me in."

"So, you just waltz right in, don't you?" she said accusingly.

"Look, I was only checking on… you clearly need help,"

De-De stood up and Kat began to laugh. Uncontrollably, she was manic. This scared De-De, and she began to walk quickly towards the door until she heard a cry that was sad and shrieking.

"Please don't leave me, I am sorry," she cried. De-De took a deep breath, already at the bedroom door, looked back and felt sorry for the woman. She seemed desperate.

De-De, went back to bed and sat next to her and noticed a stack of books on the nightstand, one of particular interest, "And Still I Rise" by Maya Angelou. She picked the book up and began to read a poem she had already read for herself several times before.

"You may write me down in history.
With your bitter, twisted lies,
You may tread me in the very dirt.
But still, like dust, I'll rise."

"Thank you for coming back, for staying," she said, resting her head on De-De's leg. De-De found herself in an unexpected space, a space between the words of Maya Angelou and a never before-seen side of a white woman. She kept reading, and Kat kept sobbing. The following Tuesday, Kat and De-De sat in their regular seats. They showed no signs of their freshly developed kinship, the crying, the vomit, nor the way De-De had stayed with Kat until sunrise of the following morning, reading to her, consoling her, encouraging her to rise. *Just like dust,* De-De thought when she first saw Kat walk into Dr. Murphy's classroom.

EMMA

Emma and Ruth had spent most of the day laughing, pulling weeds, and spraying each other with the water hose. It was a lovely Saturday, all in the company of Emma's cat named Jupiter. Ruth and Tom broke up the week before and it freed up Ruth's time now, time spent mostly with Emma. After feeling tired of the sun, the two of them went to Emma's bedroom, where Ruth sat at the edge of the bed.

"Wynona Ryder, do you think she's pretty? Tom says she's his celebrity crush and I am nothing like her," she replied, while stuffing a powdered donut in her mouth– the two of them were watching the movie Beetlejuice.

"Yes, I think so, but I don't think you should compare yourself to some celebrity who stars in movies; it is all fantasy.

"Do you think she is prettier than me?"

Emma felt the perspiration form beneath her arms before saying,

"No, no, I don't think so. You are prettier because I know you, and you are smart and kind and have the best hair!"

Ruth's face broke into a wide grin, "you are always so kind, Emma, I wish Tom spoke of me like you do."

"Does he not? "Emma hopingly asked.

"Ha-ha, we barely talked at all; all we did was have sex. If he spoke like you, we probably wouldn't have broken up!" Ruth, unaware that she had donut dust on her face, laughed.

Emma felt as if she were floating. For once, she felt as if she could compare herself to Tom. Be better than Tom, with her words at least. With her head perfectly aligned with the pillow, she allowed herself to relax into the feeling, letting contentment overwhelm her heart.

Ruth moved beside her, their arms touched, closing the gap between them. She began to rub her bare legs, almost as if to a melody, in a slow rhythmic fashion, and Emma, with lustful eyes, watched.

"I don't know why we have to shave our legs; men don't, we do all the shaving, trying to make everything so smooth, and they never do anything for us."

Emma felt a tightness in her chest, "True, but then again, I never shave."

Ruth gasped, "Never?" she said.

"It's not like I have anyone to shave for," Emma replied, "Want to see?"

"You're an adult woman!"

"Yea, an adult that doesn't show her legs," Emma exclaimed.

"Want to see?"

"Sure, I guess", said Ruth. Curiously. Emma lifted the fabric of her long skirt and revealed her pale legs, which were covered with tiny brown hairs, like the fuzz of a peach.

"Can I touch it?" Ruth asked, reaching out her hand.

"Yeah, I guess, if that is your thing," Emma replied. Ruth leaned forward, her finger touching the fine hairs that overwhelmed the length of Emma's legs and exhaled.

"Wow, reminds me of Toms, but softer," she said before retracting her hand.

"Emma? Have you ever had sex?" Ruth turned her body to face Emma and now was inches from her face.

"What are we fifteen?"

"Have you?"

"No," Emma said, embarrassed.

"I have used some things, and I think what I have felt is like sex."

Ruth, wanting more details, asked, "What things?"

"You wouldn't want to know; it's not as interesting as what you and Tom do or did."

"Show me." Ruth said with inquisitive eyes.

The following Sunday, Emma sat with her family near the back row in church, and watched as other churchgoers made their way inside. Her mother, considered a sister of the church, leaned over the back of the pew before them and whispered into another sister's ear. Her hand was on the woman's shoulder. Emma knew that her mother was praying for her and wondered what sort of problems the woman was having. *Was it her son again? Had he gotten back on drugs? Was her husband stepping out again?*

While it was not good practice to know the details of a church member's personal life, to gossip, her mother had a way of getting such private information out of people. And she would then come home to Emma after her "ministry," and tell her about it and the importance of giving grace and keeping the women she ministered to in their prayers. In a southern "bless her heart" sort of way.

"Not everyone is fortunate like us, Emma; we have to set an example of how things should be," her mother had once told her. Emma, during the exchange, thought to herself that there is never a real example of how people should be.

Despite her mother not knowing it, she learned of her mother's own affair with one of the Church brothers, who used to sit next to the pastor during Sunday service. He stopped attending shortly after the affair was exposed.

While the affair happened years ago when Emma was just a child, she remembers how they stopped attending Church and how her father began to act as if her mother did not exist; barely looking at her and avoiding sitting at the dinner table during family meals. He walked around the house as if he were searching for something—-something that he knew could never be found. Hopelessly.

"Her mother slept with the Church brother, and my mom says that she will burn in hell because she committed adulting," her classmate whispered behind Emma's back during recess. Emma dealt with the feeling of embarrassment independently, never letting on that she knew of the affair. Her father and mother now looked each other in the eyes, shared laughs, and were often affectionate. *All to the Glory of God.*

"God heals, repairs, and is always protecting us from the evil ways of this world." The pastor, the one and only pastor that Emma had ever known, said as he made his way to the podium. His ginger hair cut short, military-style, gave him a no-nonsense look as he adjusted his robe and turned the pages of his very large, gold-outlined bible. The attendees stood, clapping the tambourine and piano, *Feeling the spirit*.

The musicians and choir quickly began to slow the tempo of the music when the First Lady walked forward and placed a glass of water on the small stool that rested next to the podium. She straightened her wide-brim hat and took her usual seat. Emma watched as her mother squeezed her father's hand and brought it to her lips for a kiss.

"God," said the pastor, "is always waiting for us."

He wiped his forehead, already shiny with sweat and oil.

"God," he continued, "Needs us to allow Him into our hearts so that we can see that it is full of sin."

Having never felt uncomfortable by the pastor's words before, it required Emma a great deal of energy to remain seated as she pictured Ruth's long fingers caressing her legs. Ruth touched her in ways she had never been touched, and now she wanted to be anywhere other than eye to eye with the man preaching of damnation.

"Are we ready today to hear this message and allow Him into our hearts? Let us bow our heads and pray so that he may bless the words that I preach and so that you find truth in the word of God."

Emma watched as everyone bowed their heads before also bowing on her own. Images of the previous weekend, vivid, for she had shown Ruth exactly how she used the Russian doll, and it flashed through her mind. Emma imagined the way Ruth watched for a moment and then timidly lifted her fingers to the place that Emma touched.

She trembled and felt a rush of shivers up and down her spine. "What does that feel like?" Ruth said softly.

"It feels good," said Emma, "It feels really good.

"Lay back," Ruth replied, and Emma quickly closed her legs.

"What?" Emma's face was red.

"I mean, lay back. I'm going to show you something."

"You mean, like what you and Tom do?"

Rather than answering, Ruth slid her hands onto Emma's thighs.

"Close your eyes."

JO

Jo watched as the man spun the tire of her bicycle around. He pressed his rough fingers against the rubber until he found what he was looking for, the smooth surface of a nail.

"There it is" the man said, "I don't know how but I get more kids coming round here with nails in their bicycles than anything else."

Jo, surprised to be referred to as a kid, hunched over a bit to place her hands upon her knees, she wanted to get a better look at it.

"Yea, well wouldn't it be nice if the city and everyone chose to take care of our roads. It's nearly impossible to ride my bike, the sidewalks are horrendous." Jo said, still hunched over, while the man beside her—pale, with veiny hands—- pulled the nail out with a plier-like tool. He bit his bottom lip, and spat black goo, while he worked.

"It's bent," he said, showing the dull nail to Jo.

"Rusty?" she asked.

"Yeap almost always is. Lots of construction going on round here, aint no small town feel here no more. Louisiana really isn't that big, just packed with a bunch of crawfish and bullshit." The man let out a wheezy laugh.

"How much do I owe you?" asked Jo.

Still eyeing the rusted nail, he looked her up and down, and studied her dingy white converse shoes, ripped shorts and oversized T-shirt.

"Well, this time I won't charge you," he said, "I had nothing better to do today, anyway."

"Alright," Jo paused, and took a moment to recall his name, "Theo! Thanks for the solid, but I am still going to pay."

"You really don't have to." Theo said, waving his hand.

"Here's a five? How's that?"

"More than what I was going to charge, so it'll make do," said the man.

Satisfied, Jo took the handlebar from Theos hands and hopped on her bike.

"See you next time" she said, as she rode off, pedaling hard to make it to the grocery store before nightfall.

The man waited for Jo at the entranceway of her apartment building. His brown skin glistened in the sun, shiny as if his face had been rubbed down with oil & sheen. Age had made the man an example. His crow's feet and droopy lips revealed his age to be about sixty-five. The multi-colored windbreaker that clung loosely to his body moved at the slightest breeze, sticking to the skin of his thin arms. He was Jo's father, an addict who had left Jo's mother with the total weight of the responsibilities of raising a child.

He appeared much different from how she had imagined him in her mind all the years before. The last time she saw him, she was seven years old, and after a while, he was just a mirage of a man, a collection of features she'd make up to fill the blank spaces, created by his absence.

"She's still here," her mother said to him, "Lives in those apartments on Myrtle St, about five blocks from here."

"Hi, Jo," he said. As if he hadn't disappeared, as if he had been in her life all along and that his presence wasn't entirely unbelievable. Jo stood before him, her long legs shifting with discomfort to balance the weight of the bags she carried. She too responded, as if she had expected him to be standing there all along and she signaled for him to help with the bags.

"If it weren't for you looking exactly like me, I wouldn't know who you are."

Jo's face broke into a wide grin; she couldn't help herself; she was suddenly a seven-year-old girl smitten with her father, wanting his attention.

"It's so great to see you smile," he said, his forehead tight with excitement, his yellow teeth, crooked, protruding from his mouth as if there weren't enough space for them.

"How did you get my address?" Jo asked him, struggling to get her groceries indoors.

"Your mom, I went to the only place I knew, and she said that you might still live here; I had to try. I had to try to see you."

"How is mom?" Jo said, her face still flushed from the afternoon sun.

"Well, you know, she is still your mother. I'll tell you that," he said accusingly.

"Yea, I can imagine; I was planning on visiting soon," said Jo, though she had no real intentions of doing so. In the same city but lifestyles apart, she and her mother did best when they loved from a distance.

When the two of them finally made it into the apartment, Jo sat her bags down on the countertop, and her father quickly followed after her. She walked around her small apartment, picking up trash and the crumbled-up pieces of paper that she had left from the night before. She was embarrassed at the way her apartment looked, afraid that he would judge her messiness.

"So," they said in unison. Each of them laughed and sat down.

"What are you doing right now?" Her father asked. "Your life?"

"Well, right now, I'm still in school, actually. I know, I should already have my degree by now." Jo answered, feeling embarrassed that she was so behind and as if he could sense her embarrassment, her father cleared his throat.

"I don't know where you got it, your smarts, definitely not from me, but only a few people finish college. You should be proud."

Jo's face lit up. "Yea," she said, "This is the final semester. I've got a few plans."

"Oh yea, what's that?"

"Well, I'm going to quit working at the hotel, eventually move, for sure."

"Move? The problem with moving is that you going to take yourself with you!" her father chuckled, "Don't plan on that fixing you problems."

"I definitely don't expect that." Jo said, slightly annoyed by his response.

Jo didn't know why her father had visited her, and while she found herself to be skeptical of his true intentions, she couldn't help but trust him willingly. Jo wanted to believe that he was there out of remorse, love, to say that he was proud of who she had become. Or rather whom she was becoming.

"Are you seeing anyone? Gotta boyfriend?"

"Me? Nah." Jo said, "I don't date men, dad. I date women, I am gay."

"Oh," her dad replied.

"And it's still no, dad." she said, "I haven't been looking either."

"No one?"

"No one, dad." Jo responded.

Though it was entirely possible for Jo to make love to women, and care for them in the way that they deserved, they somehow always wanted more.

"You're going to be alone, and it will be your fault. You won't let anyone love you!" a woman she dated once told her.

"You're never here. Where are you?" said another, after sex. "You're always in your mind."

It always ended the same because Jo wanted to be with a woman that made her feel compelled. Compelled to create art. It had become a compulsion. And if Jo didn't, didn't feel compelled to create art just by the sound of a woman's voice, their body—- to be completely consumed by the intricacies of their womanhood and intellect, then she couldn't trust herself. Her feelings. She didn't believe that the "love" she was experiencing was real. Jo's idealism about love, probably on account of childhood trauma, had left her in a continuous cycle.

What's the difference between love and being in "muse." Jo thought to herself. Knowing there was a very clear difference.

"The way I see it," she said to her father, "most of the women I admire were poets, writers, and painters—and they ended up alone, too. Their work still remains though. Their words, and paintings still chariots of a version of love— unrequited, or not."

"You'll find the right one. She'll come into your life when you least expect it and change everything. That's how I felt about your mother." He spoke.

"A person has to be taught how to love, and most importantly taught how to accept love. Hadn't ever been taught, Hector." Jo said, now frustrated at how positive he was about her love life.

"Oh, using my real name now?"

Jo sat across from him with her arms crossed, even more upset that he hadn't caught on to what she said.

DR. MURPHY

Dr. Murphy was still ignoring her husband. He didn't know it, but she was. When he called, she stared at the phone in resentment and then with yearning. It helped too that she managed to keep herself busy, by going to the university's library to find literature written by a Black, impressionable writer. While she had read and studied many, she thought it would be time well spent to look at all the options at the university library. After placing a book back onto a shelf, she saw Jo sitting at the wood tables in the middle of the library. Curly hair, oversized sweater, Dr. Murphy paid attention to all the intricate details in the sweaters design before quickly making her way to the African American section of the library. It was only a moment or two before she felt someone tap on her shoulder.

It was Jo.

"Hi, Jo. How are you?" Dr. Murphy responded after she took two steps back, which encouraged Jo to take two steps forward. Closing the gap.

Dr. Murphy held her breath, feeling the sensation of a million cool fingertips on the back of her neck.

"I am fine; how are you?" Jo spoke, flipping through the pages of the book she had just bought.

Dr. Murphy's eyes darted around the room, she appeared to be distracted.

"Are you ok?" said Jo, as she looked at Dr. Murphy up and down, from head to toe.

Dr. Murphy's white blouse was reflected in the light of Jo's eyes. It was unbuttoned just a bit, allowing Jo to see the moles on Dr. Murphy's neck that were perfectly aligned, like constellations.

Jo had a way of making her feel uncomfortable, flushed even. In fact, most of their interactions were awkward and if by chance Jo walked beside Dr. Murphy while in conversation, Dr. Murphy would gallop. Her steps were quick, she was always in a rush. In a rush to get away from Jo—despite wanting to remain close.

"Yes," she said, "I am doing great!"

"Good." Jo replied before turning to walk away feeling uneasy with their interaction. However, she did want to ask Dr. Murphy a question and so she quickly turned around.

"Dr. Murphy?"

"Yes"

"I am interested in writing. Do you have any tips? What could I do to get better, be better?"

Dr. Murphy shifted the strap to the bag that dug into her shoulder. "Read more," she said with an emotionless face. "Read more?" Jo asked back, "Yes."

Unsure of how to respond, Jo spoke again, "Thanks, I get the hint," and turned to walk away. Dr. Murphy inhaled deeply as Jo's brown legs made their way in the opposite direction, and without any hesitation, she called out, "Hey! Do you have any suggestions for our next class? Subjects, or themes, you think the class would be interested in. I'm thinking of assigning reading for extra credit."

She tried her best to speak in as neutral of tone as she could. Jo at once stopped walking and turned back.

"Well, I don't know if you are interested, but maybe Minnie Bruce Pratt?"

"We Say We Love Each Other." She is over in the miscellaneous section, by the F's, even though none of the authors' names begin or end with an F. At least I do not think so. A few of my friends keep the best books close together; it's like a secret society. If you can't find a copy, I have one. Let me know!"

"What is it about?" Dr. Murphy, genuinely curious, asked. Hoping it would keep Jo standing before her for a bit longer,

"Well, you'll just have to see for yourself. I think you will like it!" she said before turning and walking away, yet again.

Secret Society? Dr. Murphy thought.

She was interested in learning what type of books Jo read, which ones made her stay up late at night, and got beneath her skin. *What books make her throw her head back, or throw it down in disbelief? What sort of books inspire her?*

Dr. Murphy waited until Jo was out of sight and went to the miscellaneous section of the library, fumbling over her feet. Her nerves were shot for no apparent reason and after reading the blurb on the back of she concluded that the book was a lesbian title. She shoved the book into her bag without bothering to check it out, not embarrassed that she had it in her hand, but embarrassed that her student recommended it. That Jo had recommended it.

At home Dr. Murphy checked her answering machine for missed calls and listened to the desperate plea of Bennette. "You're going to have to call him up sometime, August" she said to herself just before searching her leather bag for the book that Jo recommended and reading the very first page she turned to. "Peach" and it read:

"My tongue, your ass:
the center of a peach,
ripe, soft, pitted, red-fibbed flesh,
dissolving toward earth, lust.
Eat you? I ask."

Dr. Murphy gasped, she could not believe that Jo would suggest such a thing, however, she felt compelled to continue flipping through the pages until her eyes fell on another titled,

"Not the End of the Story." Dr. Murphy began to read:

"...Lying on you naked, naked skin to skin,
as on damp ground in the early evening or at the
bottom of a well that seeps cool water sweat at
summer's dry end.
The candle burns down low, a blue methyl beryl.

Flame deep in the well. In the story, the witch said, dig up my garden, split my wood, go fetch my blue light that never goes out, lost in the well.

Deep under me, you breathe out words to catch my hands. The night fills up with rain, a soft risk. Against the brick walls of the sky. You sleep.

The flame is shaking blue, my last pleasure of the night: to watch with my face sideways on your breast, your skin calm as wet dirt under me, to go to sleep before the candle goes out. "

She read the poem with intrigue and absolute longing before quickly closing the book.

The next day in class, Jo sat in the back row with a big smile. Knowing that the book she had suggested to Dr. Murphy was a lesbian one, a lesbian erotic, full of complex lesbian poetry, and she could hardly wait to see Dr. Murphy's reaction or lack thereof. When Dr. Murphy walked into the class, she tapped Jos' desk while walking towards the podium as if to say, "Hello."

Maybe she hasn't read it yet, Jo thought.

"Today, we will be going over the works of a bestselling author, Glory Jackson Smith, "said Dr. Murphy, emphasizing each part of the author's name. "Glory Jackson wrote the short story "Red Lips," and was critically acclaimed after the short story was published in the New Yorker. I printed out photocopies, and we will read an excerpt before watching one of her interviews."

Jo watched as Glory Jackson Smith ran her hands through her long braids, and smiled each time she saw Glory Jackson Smiths freckled cheeks rise high on her face with excitement. Glory Smith was a middle-aged mixed woman from London who published her first book at the age of twenty-five and Jo was completely and utterly amazed. Experiencing for the first time the sweet relic of representation; of seeing someone who quite literally looked like her, talk about the very thing that kept her held together like glue, writing.

Jo stared at the screen completely enchanted. *How had I never heard of her before?* Glancing over at Dr. Murphy, who was giggling in response to Glory Jackson Smith's responses, Jo felt extremely thankful.

Learning about Glory Jackson Smith had ignited something within Jo, something that she hadn't felt since she was a teenager—-she was inspired. She wanted to begin to take writing seriously again. It was obvious to her that "Written Word" was her truest love. The two, together in "holy matrimony" since Jo first proclaimed to want to be an author at the ripe age of nine.

"Ya'll can leave once you turn the assignment in?" Dr. Murphy said with nearly thirty minutes of class time remaining. One of the last to complete the assignment, Jo turned to Dr. Murphy on the way out.

"Did you enjoy Minni?"

"Yes, she... her work, it is interesting." Dr. Murphy answered, never meeting Jo's eyes and Jo couldn't tell if Dr. Murphy was upset about the book or not.

"I really loved today's lesson," she said to Dr. Murphy, "See you next class."

"Good, I knew you would," Dr. Murphy said, still gathering her belongings. Jo was captivated by her diction, the very specific tone of her voice. Mesmerized, the moment Dr. Murphy fixed her mouth to say anything at all, Jo stood before her a bit longer. It wasn't until the two of them began to walk towards the door at the same time, that they realized one of them had to slow down or they would collide.

"Jo, do you have a moment?" Dr. Murphy asked, almost in a whisper.

"Sure," Jo said.

"I appreciate your suggestion, Pratt?" Dr. Murphy spoke again, knowing very well who the author was.

"Yes!" Jo said.

"Well, I stumbled upon this book... A while ago, I thought you might like it."

"Really, thank you!" Jo's face lit up. "Thank you for thinking of me."

"Sure, no problem," Dr. Murphy said, offering her first genuine smile of the day. The two of them spoke without having to share a single word.

"Ok, see you later!" Jo said, her feeling of gratitude mountainous. She reached out her hand to shake Dr. Murphy's, and Dr. Murphy stood lifeless as she listened to the little voice in her head. *"No physical contact with students."*

This in turn made Jo retract. Taking a step back, she brushed the palm of her hands against the pocket of her cargo pants. A place deep within her ached. How could a woman she hardly knew affect her in that way? All she wanted to do was crawl under Dr. Murphy's gaze—to be an arm's length away, to experience the sort of intimacy she'd never be able to vocalize but only express through poetry.

What is wrong with me?

"One more thing, Jo," Dr. Murphy blurted out.

"Check out pg.17"

"Ok, I will. For sure, "she said, trying to avoid looking into Dr. Murphy's eyes. Jo's insides, a ravenous wolf, ready to consume the literature. To her, the book recommendation, especially from Dr. Murphy, fulfilled some deep need.

Several hours later, at Kat's apartment, Vita and De-De sat on Kats' bed. The three of them had grown closer after one solid moment of connection at a greasy burger joint two weeks prior. The joint famously had the greasiest, most disgustingly, well-cooked burgers, and as each of them sat around each other stuffing their faces, watching as sauce and cheese slid down the opening of their mouths a bond was formed; Of course, women amongst candid conversation and food created a sort of magic.

De-De liked them, Vita and Kat, which was something she hadn't anticipated.

"Is it hard being a single mother?" Vita asked Kat, still on the bed. She could not help but feel judgmental when she asked her, even though the question came from honest curiosity. She couldn't imagine being in Kat's shoes.

"I mean, being a single mother is what makes you so…" Vita continued, when Kat did not respond.

"Depressed?" Kat spoke, looking down at her nail beds, her fingernails that were once painted red, had chipped horribly.

"No," she continued, "The kids certainly make me more depressed.... among countless other things," she said as she braided a long strand of her blonde hair.

"It's that I feel I have no control; it's like two little humans have all the control, and there is nothing that I can do about it. I can't just wake up and go for a jog; I can't just stay in my pajamas all day and write. I can't randomly read a book or even randomly fuck a guy. I can't just think of myself, not when it comes to dinner, travel, a shower, nothing at all. Motherhood taught me how selfish I can be. Not that there's anything wrong with selfishness, is there?" Kat asked before continuing.

"Don't make the food too spicy, don't say yes to a date, don't start writing that novel! Why? Because I will never have time to finish it. I may be wrong, but I think my depression stems from feeling as if I can't be myself, apart, solo, and the freedom of being an individual. Something that I have always valued in entirety," Kat continued.

"I used to feel as if there were endless possibilities, and now there is only one possibility, motherhood. I've always been depressed; it is just now that I have had children; the darkness, I like to call it, won't accept that it can no longer come first. Nothing comes before the children. Not even me." She said, looking in the direction of De-De.

"I hate being a mother!"

"HATE? Well, why did you choose to have them?" De-De asked.

"The guilt? I could never live with myself if I got an abortion, or at least that is what I thought. Sometimes, I feel like I ruined my life. And that is God's honest truth. I am still angry at the reasons I chose to go along with it. Twice."

De-De now feeling sorry for the two white kids eating their snacks in the next room, said, "Look, don't take this personally, but what I think you HATE is that you haven't finished your novel, I think you hate that you didn't travel, I think you hate that you keep giving your heart to lames, I think you hate....yourself?"

Vita's mouth dropped open. Kat stopped braiding. For a moment, it seemed that their newly developed friendship would instantly be broken, but then Kat said to De- De, "Maybe you're right. Maybe I hate myself and all my stupid choices, and I am just projecting."

De-De continued, "Write, take trips, get on trains, go on hikes with your kids, read the stack of books that you have had sitting on your nightstand for ages. Separate yourself from your traumas."

"I have to face my traumas every day!" Kat exclaimed with a smile.

"Hell, your house is a mess anyway, you might as well let it be a mess because you are doing what you want. And that asshole you're dating, let him go, you don't need some man that leaves you waiting...."

They all started to laugh. They laughed at how serious the conversation had become and how as teenagers, they never saw themselves becoming adults, navigating their way through serious situations.

"Who would have ever thought we'd be here listening to De-De's pep talk," said Vita.

"When did we all become so serious?"

To change the subject, Kat asked, "What do you guys think of Jo? "

"She is alright, I like her style; I heard she writes well too," said De-De.

Vita laughed, "I think that she likes our professor; she's obviously her favorite, too."

De-De and Kat gasped.

"She's taken, what? Four of her classes?" Vita asked.

"Ha, ha," Kat joined, "Dr. Murphy is as straight as a board, I heard that her husband is a very talented chef! She isn't into women."

"I think she's only taken two. Actually."

"MAYBE," Vita said and turned to page one seventy-six in their textbooks; the others followed.

VITA

Vita, in the kitchen with her mother, felt disturbed. As she washed the dishes, she couldn't help but reflect on the last evening she and Grayson spent together. It was the second day of fall break and one and a half weeks since she had spoken to him. In the soap suds, she saw everything that was wrong with their relationship. The way he laughed her ambitions off, wanted every minute of her attention to himself, hardly ever offered a solid opinion about her written work. Which would not have been a problem had she not known the truth, which was that he simply didn't care enough to have an opinion.

Still Vita couldn't help but to think of everything that Grayson did right. The way he made her laugh, his enthusiastic interest in Biology, and the way that he had made her feel physically. Her mother, upon noticing the way Vita stood in a daze at the kitchen sink, went up to her and asked, "How are you holding up?"

"I don't know, Mom," she said while rinsing off a plate.

"In some ways, I feel as if I am doing everything right, and in others, I feel like I am entirely failing."

Her mother stepped closely beside her and spoke quietly,

"Do what feels right. Do you want to talk to Grayson? Then call. Do you want to break up and never see him again? Then do that, and then go spend your life doing what you want. Even if it means never getting married or having children."

Vita, surprised at her mother's response, said,

"It is not about him, Mom; not everything is about a man, or marriage."

"Oh, but in this case, it is," her mother said.

Vita continued, "And even if it were, what if what I feel is wrong? Everyone is so concerned about me getting married. What if he is right, what if going to grad school isn't fulfilling, what if writing isn't my thing."

Vita's mother took the dripping dish from Vita's hand.

"Your father told me what happened, Vita, and well, you have always gone in the direction of your heart; no need to stop now. And for that, whether you know it or not, I am proud. I can finish the dishes; thank you for helping."

Vita reached up and touched her mother's shoulder, for she had never been comforted like this before. Not from her mother.

"Are you happy? Do you feel happy with the choices you have made?"

Her mother, the perfect wife, cook, and socialite, kept drying the dishes. Vita stood looking at her, waiting for a reply. Nothing, her mother said nothing at all.

Vita took a deep breath and exhaled, uncertain of why she had dared to ask her mother that. They had never been that honest with one another before, but just as she turned away to walk towards the room, her mother said, almost as if it were a secret.

"I made the choices that I felt I had to make." She knew that her lifestyle disappointed Vita. A woman whose only title was Mother could never be admirable to someone like Vita. She took note of the way her daughter watched her with disdain, the exasperated glances Vita often gave her while she prepared the family's meals and cleaned their home.

Her husband was the one who made the money, made the decisions, and was the one that Vita idolized. And the one that her sons would grow up to emulate. Vita's mother knew that her circumstances, her relationship with Vita, were the result of a role well played.

What Vita did not know, however, is that her mother, too, was just like her once. She had dreams and aspirations and questioned things, too, all of which were intercepted by secrets, shame, and regrets.

Church meetings, being the mother who was always on time, with homemade baked goods for her children's classroom; it was all a ruse, a disguise, one great way to hide the simple truth that Vita wasn't her husband's biological child. It was something she had intended to keep secret for the rest of her life, doing any and everything to avoid being noticed or questioned. Vita's mother swore twenty years prior that she would be the best wife and mother to avoid all suspicions.

Vita left the kitchen without any validation, and after being unable to get her mother's words out of her head, nor those of Grayson, paced in her bedroom. The wood floor creaked beneath her weight. It was fall break; she could have been writing, making plans for after graduation, and yet it was all she could do but obsess over why she felt so confused, alienated, and unsure of her future.

Vita knew deep down that it shouldn't matter what Grayson said to her; of course, he had proven to her his true character, had confirmed that his chivalry, his whole persona was a fallacy. She never fully trusted him, his intentions; he simply wanted to capture the one woman that didn't grow weak in the knees anytime he announced his presence. And yet she *still* wondered if she was the actual problem in their relationship.

"But what about Mother? What about the choices she had to make?" Vita said out loud as she continued to walk in circles.

As far as Vita knew, her mother was exactly who she always wanted to become and had only ever made the choices she wanted to make.

DE-DE

De-De hadn't heard from Kat, who was skipping class more frequently than before. She walked up to Kats' apartment holding bags of chips for her children, and a cd titled, "Supposed Former Infatuation Junkie," an album she thought that Kat might like. The door was quickly answered by a shirtless white man with more chest hair than De-De had ever seen.

"Hi, is Kat here?" De-De asked, eyeing the hair on the man's chest. He had kind eyes, and rather than answering her he just opened the door wider. Which allowed De-De to see inside. "Smells like someone is in a great mood," De-De said loudly as she walked in with her gifts. Kat turned, striking, she was dressed up with a face full of makeup.

"Oh, hi," she said, almost too happily.

"How are you, friend? my best friend, De-De Johnson. This is the friend I was telling you about!" Kat spoke without taking a breath.

"Is that so? nice to meet you, I've heard great things!" The boyfriend said. He was charming, but De-De could see right through it, right through to the point where she saw him leaving Kat yet again in the tiny apartment with only booze and angst.

De-De's eyes searched the kitchen for the children.

"Where are the kids?" she said, attempting to change the subject.

"Oh, they are napping," Kat said with her back turned towards De-De. She was now hunched over, putting something De-De could not see into the oven.

"De-De! Would you like a drink?" asked the boyfriend.

De-De looked around at the apartment, which was, for once, perfectly clean and smelled nice. It was when she noticed a few empty beer cans and a bottle of vodka that she fully understood what was going on.

"Are you drinking again, Kat?" she asked, clearly upset.

"Look, I've only had one drink; it is not that big of a deal," she said, rubbing her hands along the seams of her dress.

De-De gritted her teeth, she fought the tears which were beginning to well up in her eyes and took a deep breath. *Nope, not today, not going to let this silly white woman make me cry, not in front of her, no way.* She put the CD and bag of chips down on the kitchen table and angrily made her way towards the parking lot of Kat's apartment building. Refusing to feel what she had truly felt only moments before, sadness, De-De walked as if Kat had never existed. *She never added anything of value to my life anyways.*

The very next day De-De sat towards the front of a Greyhound bus headed towards Augusta, Georgia. It had been a year since she last visited home. She missed her family, her mother's hands, her father's face, his stone, focused gaze, and her grandmother's scent; honeysuckles and sweat. She could already taste the hot-water cornbread, squash, and perfectly marinated oxtails because the bus ride had left her hungry. Her mouth began to water at the thought of the meat quickly falling away from the bone.

When she finally arrived, they welcomed her with warm embraces. Her grandmother, even at eighty years old, still tended to the yard, smelled like she always had. A woman laboring her way to personal satisfaction, as opposed to the satisfaction of others.

Just as De-De had imagined, her family had prepared a meal, and she was more than happy to indulge–De-De sat around the table with the family members her mother opted to invite over. The short visit had turned into a large family reunion. She ate with Aunts and Uncles she hadn't seen in ages, her little cousins ran around with colored ribbons and barrettes in their braided hair, while the little boys with high tops and low fades played with sticks and paper planes in the front yard. This of course all happened whilst Anita Baker,

Dianna Ross, and Louis Armstrong blasted in the background.

"How would it end? Isn't got a friend.
My only sin is in my skin.
What did I do to be so black and blue?"

Louis Armstrong sang, his voice just the right amount of soul.

De-De found herself, just for a moment wishing she had never left; how wonderful it felt to be in the presence of rounded, black, moon-shaped faces. High cheekbones, beautiful wide noses, and coils that reached up towards the sun that looked like her own. For her, nothing could replace the feelings that came with commonality, community.

However, the sense of community De-De coveted, quickly turned into drama. See, it was a sort of family tradition that the men, at most of their gatherings, settle somewhere and play spades and they did so accordingly up until the very moment her Aunt Moira came in, drunk and yelling. Suddenly, disturbing the peace. She was yelling at De-De's uncle Ernest, who apparently had been cheating on her with their neighbor. The two had been married for over twenty years, but her Uncle Ernest had a habit of stepping out. It certainly wasn't the first time that a neighbor's child was allegedly his.

"Ya just a no-good fool, willing to stick it in anything," her Aunt Moira confronted him.

De-De's Uncle Ernest just sat there, taking a long swig of his Hennessy.

"Woman aint nobody slept with nobody, I aint got the time," he said, adjusting his tan fedora; the man looked up at Moira as if she had lost her mind, and continued to play his hand.

"Woman, you are stirring up trouble. You're crazy!" he said.

"Yes, you did, Ernest, yes you did, she told me, you ain't no good and never will be," She yelled and went right up to his face and with her index finger, poked his forehead repeatedly and said, "Poking, poke, poke, Mr. Ol' poke her," her gold bracelets clunk together just as passionately as she poked his forehead.

De-De's Uncle Ernest, aggravated, threw his cards down.

"Yeah, I'll poke you if you keep on."

That is when De-De's mother intervened, and even though her mother was the youngest of five when she spoke, everyone listened. She had natural authority, something she had passed on to De-De.

"Will, you two shut up, my baby is home, and lord knows when she will come again, mama is s...."

De-De's mother stopped speaking and looked at De-De, before saying, "Just calm down; now is not the time."

Uncle Ernest looked at his mother, De-De's grandmother, before apologizing.

"I'm sorry, mama, the way we are acting, it's not right."

The energy shifted, what was once a lively family function turned into a solemn, sunken place.

De-De still, sitting next to her grandmother and tired of the drama, reached over to squeeze her grandmother's hands, which were arthritic and warm. Her grandmother squeezed back with a loose arthritic squeeze.

"Some things change, and some things never change at all, be the change baby," her grandmother whispered.

De-De smiled that was her cue to exit. "And with that, I'll excuse myself," she said, and left to go to her old bedroom. Laying in her old bed, she looked around at everything that symbolized who she had once been. They had never changed her room; they kept everything in its place. Her poster of Grace Jones, Malcolm X, her awards from high school competitions, and her comforter were all the same, but there she was, lying there, completely different. *It's all the same, but I've changed.* De-De thought.

KAT

It was nighttime when he made it to her apartment and found her to be still awake. Her boyfriend lightly knocked on her door, and Kat opened just as far as the chain link would allow.

Her eyes were squinted as if she could barely keep them open, while she struggled to maintain balance.

"I've been calling you all night," he said to her, still trying to open the door.

"Little Ol' me??" Kat asked while disconnecting the chain with shaky hands. When she finally got it unhooked and stepped back to let him in, he saw her tiny body moving in a slow sway, bare-chested, with her hair sticking out in every direction. Kats eyeliner smudged, ran down her cheeks, the track marks of tears.

The two of them stood before one another, looking still near her apartment door.

"Care to come in?" Kat asked, swaying, as she rubbed her eyes. He said yes, and watched as Kat stepped over toys, clothes, and other things that he could not make out in the low light of the living room.

"Are you drunk?"

"Ha-ha, now that is funny, ha-ha, me, drunk, noooooooooooooo," Kat said, innocent and child-like, like a schoolgirl with a crush. "What a stupid question!" She held up a nearly empty bottle of alcohol.

"Want some?" she asked.

"I'm good, and I think you're good too," he said and tried to take the bottle from her. She held onto the two of them tightly, unyielding.

"Let it go, let it go now; you either take a shot with me, or you can leave," she yelled. He didn't let it go, and so she got louder, "you can just show up when you want and tell me what to do."

He had never seen that side of her before; he had never seen any of it. Not the state of her apartment, her face fixed in rage, teeth gritted together like those of a rabid dog, but he could see it then, even in the dim light.

"You're the reason I drink!" Kat exclaimed.

"Look, I don't know what is going on, but if you need help or something is wrong, I can help you." He said while trying to pull her close.

She refused his embrace, "I don't need you; get out. You use me for a good time and now you're standing there judging me?"

It was when he attempted to grab the bottle again that she began to scream, and this scared him. *What if someone thinks I'm trying to hurt her?* He thought while Kat kept screaming. More high-pitched, more dramatic. Unsure of what to do, he did the only thing he could do, leave Kat there, standing in her doorway while she screamed at him as he walked down the sidewalk. He felt that at any moment, cops would show up, and arrest him, for a crime he had never intended to commit.

"I am leaving, I am leaving, just calm down. You're gonna wake your kids; someone's gonna call the cops," he said, nervously stepping further away.

When he drove off and looked back into his rearview mirror, he could see her still standing there, bare breasted under the light of her porch with her mouth wide open. He watched her in his rearview until he could no longer hear the screams over the engine of his car.

He had somehow become her enabler. When he came around life was a party, but when he left, he left her alone to reflect on the emptiness, the deep void that being outside of his presence created. That being outside of anyone's presence created. "Everyone does it," De-De had told her,

"I do it too; I bury myself in schoolwork and self-isolation."

"My roommate does it with sex and pot, we all have our vices but if we aren't careful, then our vices begin to control our life. Find another vice. Make writing your vice. You love to write."

When De-De told her that, she wanted to say, "But I can't write when I am depressed," but she didn't. She was just grateful to have a friend like De-De who cared enough for her to try and think of solutions.

"You're right, I'll try," Kat told her.

When Kat finally stopped screaming, her throat was raw, sore from her screaming rage. *Fucking loser,* she thought, embarrassed that she had gone back to exactly where she started, the stumbling, throwing up, being angry and volatile.

DR. MURPHY

Dr. Murphy danced around in her living room as she listened to Tina Turner. The woman's music had a way of helping her temporarily forget her troubles, and so when the phone rang, she did not answer. Deep down she already knew it was Bennette on the other end, and preferred hearing the sound of Tina's voice.

"You're simply the best, better than all the rest," Tina Turner sang to Dr. Murphy as she spun around fast, picturing her husband and Summer laughing, their *mollejas* and sweet bread- *sweet as you.*

"Sweet as you...sweet as you" she said aloud, scrunching up her face.

"Stuck on your heart!"

Dr. Murphy struck her wood floor, hard.

"That's it. There it is!" she whispered, having enough of even herself. Dr. Murphy willed her way· towards the bedroom where she dove nose first into its plush comfort.

The next morning Dr. Murphy laid as an aching soul with a yearning that came from a peculiar dream in which she had been intimate with a woman; a pulsating ache from temptation being trapped inside for too long. With her head pounding she struggled to look around her bedroom. She wished for a moment that she could go back to sleep, to the woman, to that feeling. However, she slowly lifted herself out of bed towards the medicine cabinet and popped two Tylenol before walking into her large kitchen, and it was there that she stared at the coffee machine as it worked quickly to produce her caffeine. After two large cups of black coffee, Dr. Murphy spent the bulk of the day lounging around in her apartment, watching reruns, and eating ice cream.

Of all the disappointments in life, Mint Chocolate ice cream has never disappointed me, she thought. It was her favorite ice cream because when she was a little girl, she read a book where one of the characters had mint ice cream at their birthday party.

Immediately after reading the description of how the ice- cream tasted, according to the birthday girl, she vowed to try some. Dr. Murphy was nine at the time, and when her mother invited her to the nearest ice cream shop called "Little Chippers," she seized the opportunity to try it for the very first time. A vivid pale green with brown freckles, it melted in her mouth, offering her the best sweet pleasure she had had up until that point.

When the cool minty flavor dissolved on her tongue, she thought back to how the character described its taste. *To a T.* She hadn't strayed since and, at any instance, was willing to proclaim that it was the very best flavor that ever existed. Even though people, like her work colleagues, and other acquaintances would always stick out their tongues in disagreement.

Even as an adult, Dr, Murphy questioned if she tasted the flavor of the ice cream when she ate it, or if the words that she read as a child somehow affected her taste buds. As if the anticipation itself was enough to make her hail it as the best ice cream to ever exist. *Am I just tasting the words? Yes,* she thought, *that is how powerful they are.*

Dr. Murphy made her way towards the kitchen to refill her bowl with ice cream, and someone rang the doorbell. Somewhat annoyed, she quickly tossed her empty bowl into the sink. The doorbell rang again.

"Oh Christ, I'm coming, one minute!" she yelled.

She stuck the silver spoon with traces of mint into her mouth and closed the opening of her sheer night robe. When she turned around, she saw Bennette standing before her, leaving her no choice but to yelp and grab her chest.

"Bennette!!!" Dr. Murphy, swiped at his chest, "You nearly gave me a heart attack." He stood laughing, his chuckle comforting. She hadn't heard it in a while.

"I see some things never change," he said as he looked into the sink at the empty bowl.

"Oh, well, you know, it all started with words," she said as she tightened her robe shut.

"So, as you were saying? You are coming?" He walked towards her. Inches from her face.

He opened her robe, eyed her silky nightgown, then placed his hand on her chest right in the center so that he could feel how quickly her heartbeat. He kissed her forehead with a certain gentleness that incited anticipation.

Dr. Murphy grew wet, then thought of Summer and stepped back.

"What are you doing here?" she asked.

"As I recall, it is my home, and I don't need to make an announcement, do I?" Bennette asked, also stepping back, trying to get a good look at her. Trying to read whether she had intentionally been avoiding his calls all along.

"Well, no, not really, but it would have been better than making me go through cardiac arrest," Dr. Murphy replied, running her fingers through her brown hair.

"You are fine, and I mean really, really fine," he said deviously, placing his hands around her waist.

He always did that. Made her feel like the most magnificent being in a room, restaurant, building, wherever. Of course, she could never really relax into the feelings that he provoked, the sense of security, because she had her own suspicions about what he had done with his sue chef.

"How did you get a flight so fast?" she asked, removing his hands from around her waist. Dr. Murphy had questions and wanted him to answer them.

"I planned this months ago, and when you didn't answer the phone, I got worried."

Dr. Murphy looked down, unable to meet his charming gaze.

"I'll be leaving in two days; I have to go back," He continued to say while grabbing a freshly washed bowl, "but I missed you, so you better enjoy it while it lasts."

Bennette reached into the freezer and got out the mint chocolate Ice-cream.

"Care to join me?" he asked, always knowing what she wanted.

Later that night, after several shared glasses of wine Bennette took off Dr. Murphy's nightgown by touching it as if it were worth the weight of gold. His fingers trailed over her torso, her breast. He kissed her everywhere as if he were marking his territory, pulling her hair precisely the way she liked it before taking her in every way possible. Dr. Murphy woke up groggy, almost forgetting that Bennette had come home. When she looked over at him lying next to her and rubbed her eyes, it took her a moment to realize he was the book that Jo had suggested to her. She quickly reached to grab it from him,

"What are you doing?" Bennette moved away from her with the speed of an insolent child. "I missed you tonight; I had gone just before dark to the Garden to cut what was left of the cabbages." He teased.

"So is this why you haven't been answering my calls, reading I see, reading about Dykes."

"Oh, stop it, it was just something one of my students suggested," she told him, now sitting up in their bed. She realized how strange the statement sounded and felt a prickly sensation at the back of her neck, while Bennette stood next to the bed on the opposite side. The smell of the fresh coffee he made for her filled the room.

He stroked his dark beard and continued, "In the hollows of the red clay, there is rain and freezing,' How poetic," he said as he closed the book and tossed it beside her.

Dr. Murphy rolled her eyes.

His teasing continued until he received a phone call, leaving Dr. Murphy to blow on her freshly made coffee alone. "I better go take a shower" she said to herself as Bennette stood on the patio, his facial expression tense while he talked on the phone. *A business call?*

Dr. Murphy sat in the chair which was facing in his direction and watched as he paced back and forth; the quick way in which his mouth moved.

She could not hear him because when he stepped out onto the patio, he closed the glass sliding doors, as if he knew he needed privacy. Bennette's back was turned to her, and just for a moment she wished that he would turn around, notice her, and see how much she needed him to come inside.

The two of them had only a few more hours before his flight back to Argentina, and the lingering unrest that she had been experiencing the last few weeks remained. *Is he sleeping with Summer? Is that who he is speaking with on the phone?* Finally deciding to take a shower after all, Dr. Murphy tried her best to ignore her husband's sudden mood shift once he began to talk on the phone.

She tested the temperature with her index finger before placing her head beneath the hot water, allowing it to drench her hair and face, and then reached for the handmade soap that she had recently bought at the overly crowded farmers market two weeks prior.

Standing beneath the water with her eyes closed, and she thought about her students. All of them, until soon, she thought of only Jo. *Had she read page.17 of the book that I gave her?* She imagined Jo standing in front of her, wanting to take her hand, the images in her mind were vivid—so much so Dr. Murphy had the urge to put her hand out in front of her. It was then that she felt the cool air hit the back of her legs and opened her eyes to see Bennette standing before her, naked with a wide grin. Dr. Murphy willingly welcomed him in, allowing his body to press against hers. Deep down she knew that it would be a long time before she'd be intimate with him again.

"Do you want to get breakfast at the Bluebird?" he asked whilst Dr. Murphy fastened a braided belt around her waist.

"Sure, that sounds good," she said.

"Who were you speaking to on the phone?"

"Oh, it was just work stuff; they act like they can't manage the kitchen without me, it is chaotic," Bennette spoke, and finished putting on his shoes.

"Chaotic," Dr. Murphy repeated as if she had never heard the word before. As if it didn't perfectly describe the emotions that her all-telling intuition had left her with.

JO

When Jo was seven, her mother packed everything they could fit into an old Buick and the two of them went on a drive that seemed to have lasted for days. Her mother told her that they would start a new life away from Jo's father.

"He isn't good for us, Jo."

Her mother said to her as she loaded up the small vehicle. Jo couldn't remember much of the trip, only the feeling of hunger and the dull ache in her legs from being cramped up for too long. It wasn't until her mother needed to sleep that they pulled into the nearest parking lot where mother could find rest that she snuck out of the vehicle to stretch her own legs. Her tiny footsteps made crunching noises against the loose gravel—Jo knew she shouldn't have gotten out of the vehicle, at least without her mother's consent, but she did anyway.

Nearby, a homeless woman with large fleshy arms, stood leaning against a car parked across from theirs. The woman flicked cigarette butts, one after another, chain smoking. She didn't speak a word to Jo but watched with a parental eye as Jo paced back and forth and periodically looked into the window of the Buick where her mother slept. Even as an adult Jo, still thought of the homeless woman, wondering if she was still alive, and why the woman stood eyeing her up until the very moment she climbed back in the car with her mother.

The next morning, Jo and her mother pulled into the parking lot of an apartment complex that was painted bubblegum pink. Blue, gold, and green beads hung from the large oak tree that stood like a monument smack in the middle of the courtyard. New Orleans.

"This isn't a house!" Jo complained.

Her mother sighed, "Jo, we will get a house; we only have to stay here for a little while to get on our feet. I promise."

Josephine's eyes welled up with tears, "You promised me."

It was at that moment that Jo realized that she couldn't trust her mother, not in the way she had before, with blind naivety. Now, her father was staring at her with eager eyes, hanging on to each of her words. For Jo, it was nice to have him there, to have him listen to her aspirations with approval.

"How do you pay for this place?" Her father asked.

"I pay for it with student loans, and I have a part-time position at the hotel up the street. I mean, I'll make it okay." Jo spoke, "But I know I'll make more money when I graduate and find an actual real job."

"Good, very good," He said, "Hey, you remember when I used to make you breakfast, and you'd pour nearly the whole bottle of hot sauce on it?" He laughed, "You always like spicy stuff."

Jo did remember, but not in the same way he had.

"I do remember," she said, "Eggs. Eggs. And more eggs every day."

"I could make some for you again. Maybe some Chorizo too?" Her father said, more of a question than a statement.

"That would be great," Jo smiled. "But I don't have any eggs." It was true, in fact when she reached adulthood, she practically swore them off. The thought of eggs made her mouth water, and not in a good way.

"I'd say I had it, but I don't" he used his hands to pat his pockets.

Wanting to please her father, and feel taken care of, Jo ignored the feeling of nauseousness that had overtaken her.

"It's okay, I got it. I haven't been spending much lately. I'll give you the money, and you can go while I clean up my mess." She said, feeling as if she were a seven-year-old child again, wanting to please him so that he would stay.

"I will go straight to the market and head back."

"Okay, let's see," Josephine said, taking her wallet out of her back pocket, I got a twenty! That should be enough!"

"I don't think I need that much? Do you?" Her father said, rocking back and forth.

"Well, you can just bring me the change back?"

"What about drinks? You got something to drink in there?" he asked her.

"Got water, a few cokes? Is that good?

"I think so."

"Good." Jo replied.

Jo handed her father the twenty-dollar bill before shutting the door behind him and leaning against it. She looked around her tiny apartment, and was grateful for it, grateful to be able to close the door on people, places and situations that only made her feel heavy, weighing her spirit down.

Her father's memory had been warped; he never made her breakfast; she made him and her mother breakfast to try to wake them up, to try to keep them from sleeping the day away. She made breakfast because if she hadn't made it for herself, she would have starved.

Jo knew she would never see her father again.

She thought back to when she was four or five years old, how her parents left her for a full week with a neighbor. Every night, she'd sit on the floor in their kitchen, refusing to eat whatever food they'd offer her—hoping that her parents, her mother, would show up. Even at that age Jo knew she would spend her life waiting for something or someone to show up, save her, show that they cared.

Still leaning against the door, Jo's eyes fell onto something that peaked out from beneath one of the cushions of her couch. It took Jo several seconds to realize it was the book that Dr. Murphy had given her right before break. It was thin, the cover white and purple, "doris davenport," the book read. Jo felt a fluttering in her chest and immediately walked over to the couch to free it and turned to pg.17 to see a poem titled "Blackberry Time."

"It is easy," Jo told Dhalia several months before while helping her shelve books. "It is easy for me to pour all of my energy towards something, a goal, a book, it's like I'd rather exist where those things are than this reality, sometimes."

And there she was, once again, existing in another reality, one where she walked the length of a chain-link fence, felt the heat from the summer sun, barefoot——with blackberry juice oozing out as she picked them one by one. Jo read the text in the book, the sweetness of the words crept onto the tip of her tongue, and she wondered if Dr. Murphy had once tasted the sweetness of them too.

KAT

Kat knew she had hit rock bottom. She sat on her and her children's mustard orange couch as its unraveling seams appeared to struggle to keep together, struggling to support the weight of her frail frame and the heaviness in her heart. Trying to picture the exact moment she had given up, Kat grew frustrated, there were too many moments to choose from.

"Children who grow up with trauma, and take on the parental role as children, can sometimes grow up to behave like the children they never got to be," Kats psychotherapist told her. *"It's not your fault that you feel so behind, or like you can't handle your emotions. No one taught you to handle your emotions, and you spent your childhood handling your mother's."*

I never had a chance, Kat thought. Her own mother, with similar addictions, never stayed in one place, or with one man for too long, and she spent most of Kats' youth battling with her own demons as opposed to being a supportive mother.

Her mother would come in and out of her life, visiting wherever she had left her, and then, just when Kat got used to the idea of having a mother, the woman would disappear in the middle of the night, or while Kat was at school.

Heartbroken, Kat was incapable of putting words to the trauma her mother's antics had given her, incapable of expressing that as a child she needed attention, interaction, and stability. *I've become her; I am her.* Kat thought. *And I don't want to be her anymore.* Instead of grabbing the half-emptied bottle of vodka that sat on the coffee table, Kat reached for her purse. Knowing that at a certain point in her life, she'd have to stop looking backwards, allowing the past to stifle her growth. The traumas she endured, even as an adult, had to be let go of too. At a certain point she had to hold herself accountable for her own choices; despite.

Kat paid a babysitter and walked to the address she had found in the yellow phone book. When she entered the dingy room, everyone turned to look at her. Both men and women stood near a table that held donuts, an urn of hot coffee, and condiments.

Even the used furniture; a maroon armchair, an oversized couch with a detailed floral design, and the black plastic chairs organized to form a perfect circle, appeared to have eyes.

It was a place people went to expose their souls, in exchange for serenity and Kat stood at the entrance of the door, nervous, unable to meet the gaze of those whose conversations she interrupted by her presence. Just as she was about to turn to leave, a man in a flannel shirt and Levis walked up to her. He had kind eyes and wide-rimmed glasses, and a thin scar. A thin scar that went from the bottom of his chin up towards his left ear; the scar only accentuated his strong jawline, which made him appear more handsome than he was. *The type of jawline most men are envious of and one that most women admire.*

It was as if a surgeon had done it with the steadiest hand, and with the sharpest of scalpels. The man reached out to her with his hand, an invitation for a handshake.

"Hi, how are you?" he said. His voice was rather soft, not matching his rough exterior.

"I am Dale,"

Kat returned her hand to welcome his gesture of kindness, and their eyes met for the first time.

"I am Kat," she said, "This is my first time coming here, and I am not sure if I arrived on time."

"Anytime is a good time. We have started nothing yet," the man said, offering her a wide grin with yellowed teeth. He had either traded one addiction for another or kept one altogether. Smokers' teeth.

"Why don't you come on over and meet the gang? We don't bite," Dale had said to her.

Kat pushed her hair out of her face and adjusted the baby blue sweater she wore.

"It matches your eyes," her boyfriend whom she hadn't reached out to since the start of Fall break said to her before. Kat looked up to see a picture of Jesus along with a poster and bold block letters that read "The 12 Steps" hanging on the wall.

'Oh Jesus." she said under her breath.

DE-DE

After taking down several posters and filling a cardboard box with awards, stuffed animals, and other things that she had collected over the years, someone knocked on her bedroom door, which was open.

"Come in," she said, turning down the stereo, her old stereo. It was her mother.

"What are you doing?"

"I am just cleaning things up in here, making more space; you and Dad can turn it into a guest room, or anything really. Just trying to help you out mom."

Her mother, whose eyes darted around the room, slow and observant, rested her hands on her hips.

"Well, we always thought it was nice to keep your things up, make it like you aren't so far away," she said. And then, "What are you going to do with it? That box"

"I was thinking to see if Nyla wanted to go through it, and if not, then I can just trash it," De-De shrugged to show that letting go of the material items was not that big of a deal.

"You can't throw this away," her mother said as she reached into the box and took out a ceramic piece of artwork that De-De had made in her Junior year of Highschool.

"MOM," De-De said, in a tone that reminded her of her teenage self.

"You got to let things go," "Come on, help me take some of these things down."

Her mother was now sitting on the edge of the bed and looking down at the vase and was beginning to speak before there was another knock on the door. Her grandmother.

"You in here, bugging this Chile', come on De-De, let's go get some gloves so you can help me tend this garden; you aint not forgot how to work, have you," her grandmother said, to poke fun.

De-De, happy that her grandmother interrupted a conversation that she was sure that she did not want to have, put the box down and reached for her shoes.

"Alright," she said, "Give me a minute."

Soon De-De watched her grandmother's frail body throughout the walkways of the garden. There were turnips, cabbage, and squash that were so ripe they were falling away from the vine. Before long, there will be no harvest.

Seeing her grandmother, the sun, and the smell of earth made her sentimental, the image of her grandmother in the garden would remain just a memory.

De-De knew her grandmother was getting tired. Her usually vibrant brown eyes were now dull and rimmed with the same blue-like film old dogs got in the later stages of life. As far as De-De knew, it would be one of the last times she would see her grandmother, in her element, creating life with life.

"Granny", De-De said.

"Yes, baby," her grandmother, who was then on her knees pulling turnips, said.

"Can you teach me how to make that cabbage? The kind with the peppers and sausage?"

"Oh, of course, I'll do even better, you can make it, while I give you directions. My tired hands can do a lot, but with my vision and arthritis, I am not too sho how I can grip everything the way I need to. Now get on over here and help me pull up these greens," her grandmother said to her, her head tilted up so that De-De could see her face beneath the wide-brim straw hat.

She and her grandmother spent two hours together in her mother's large kitchen talking and making the cabbage dish. "Be sure to rinse it, baby, and make sure you add your tomatoes, sausage, and peppers first." De-De took her time to also write down the recipe after they were done, right up until it was too hard for her to keep her eyes open, yawning and "rubbing the sleep" out of her eyes. The sunlight from the nearest window crept its way around the room, gilding everything gold.

"You go and get yourself ready for bed, you worked hard today," her grandmother told her, and so she did. De-De slept the type of sleep that made her feel as if she hadn't slept at all— dreamless. The next morning, De-De rolled over and put her head beneath the pillow when she heard a loud knock on her door, her mother flung it open, letting it hit the wall. This confused De-De, for her mother never did anything with such force, such lack of patience.

"De-De," she said, "De-De baby, you've got to get up. It's your grandmother."

De-De flung the covers off her, her heart sinking in her chest.

"What, what's wrong?" she asked, now out of the bed, her bare feet deep in the thickness of the carpeted floor.

"She." ... her mother paused. "Your grandmother is no longer with us."

De-De fell to her knees.

Her grandmother died in her sleep, and when they found her body, it was cold and stiff, her arthritic hands sticking straight up in the air like she died in the midst of worship.

It wasn't the morning that De-De had expected, and nor did she expect that she'd have to say goodbye to her grandmother during Thanksgiving break, with just three days left to be there, to be home, and now the most important person to her wouldn't be there with her.

De-De stared off into space as her mother wept beside her.

DR. MURPHY

She needed to unlock the door to her office. Once inside, Dr. Murphy noticed that the peace lily she had been previously gifted was wilted, and this disappointed her. She assumed it would be fine on its own for a few days after a good watering because her office had natural light. *Should have known better.* The plants dropping limbs and shriveled blooms had somehow morphed into accusing eyeballs. After pouring a small amount of water into the plant's pot, Dr. Murphy put her bag down before sitting at her mahogany desk. With the lake in clear view, her mind drifted off to the day that she took The Five to read Kate Chopin at its edge until her thoughts settled Jo.

Deep down, Dr. Murphy knew that Jo was intrigued by her, but she was too selfish to shut down Jo's interest in the way she should have. Dr. Murphy also found Jo intriguing. She taught hundreds of classes and had seen the wide eyes of thousands of students—those that viewed her in that idealistic way. Yet, she never had the desire to reciprocate, until Jo. Dr. Murphy wanted to impress her, to possess Jo's attention, to feel the thrill of being able to express desire without ever having to speak a word. It made her feel alive and gave her something to do.

And it was selfish of Dr. Murphy, she knew, because she had no intention of giving in to whatever it was, they had been dancing around.

Am I leading her on? she thought to herself.

Or am I leading myself on?

And as if someone had changed the channel in her mind, her thoughts shifted towards Bennette. Dr. Murphy couldn't shake the idea of Bennette having an affair and didn't understand why it had bugged her so. She knew of his previous affair, and ignored it, choosing to instead withdraw herself from the situation by pretending she wasn't aware; and *did* have her own affair with the librarian. *Why is this one different?*

It had become apparent to her that if he was in fact having an affair, the one with Summer was different because he cared about her. It was concerning to her.

Having an affair with a woman for sexual pleasure is one thing, having an affair with a woman because of emotional attachment; that's a whole different ball game.

The thought of dating and finding another man haunted her. Thoughts of small talk, dates, and establishing new routines. Would she be capable of going through all of that again?

What would I do if he left me? Who would get the loft? How would we split the finances, and how would I handle the freedom?

Then, of course, there were those looming desires, those that she had always assumed only arose out of chaos, out of boredom, but were now cropping up like weeds, with a treacherous frequency.

She wondered if that was what she had wanted all along. A woman. The thought of it made her shiver, and Dr. Murphy grabbed her belongings, she had to do something, anything to distract herself.

VITA'S MOTHER

Fifty-two now, but she was once seventeen with her long legs, lathered in tanning oil sprawled out before her. It was the perfect day, with just enough of a breeze to keep she and her friends comfortable as they lay on the bank of the lake.

"Now that we are nearly done with school, I can't help but be frightened of what will come," her friend said, who was just a few feet away from her.

Vita's mother flipped over onto her stomach so that her tan would be even and closed her eyes as she pictured the life that was just around the corner. Smiling on the inside, she knew that she wouldn't follow a traditional path.

The two of them watched as their other friends swam, splashed and laughed in delight. Vita's mother, though, wasn't frightened, nor did she feel any apprehension about her future. She had decided she would apply to an all-women's university and study anthropology.

She would, or hoped, to spend the next few years after graduating studying humans in their environments, their culture, and finding answers to those philosophical questions like, "What is the purpose of life, or of forming a community?"

"Would you look at that," a boy said, looking down at her. His eyes fixated on the full length of her body, her backside.

Vita's mother turned her head to see him, him and his dark brown eyes, his broad shoulders. She had seen him before, around school, but had never held a conversation with him. The boy carried a case of Bartles and James beer and a bottle of Fireball whiskey. His left thumb had a cut, dried blood beneath its fingernail.

"Tackle and bait," the boy said, noticing that it was where Vita's mother focused her attention.

"Are you going to share that, or did you just come here to look pretty?" the girl lying next to Vita's mother asked him. "I might, I just might, if Miss Academia here wants some," he said with a boyish grin.

"Oh, come on, everyone knows Claudia doesn't drink," the girl said. And it was true Vita's mother, Claudia was the only one in her friend group who didn't drink and was often referred to as "The sober one."

"Well, we are almost done with our schooling now, Claudia, come on," he said. Claudia, then sitting up, agreed, "I suppose you are right, maybe I should celebrate," before lifting her hand to get served.

That next morning, she was woken up nearly naked by a dying fire. Her bikini top, still in one piece, covered her breast, but her bottoms were ripped at her hip, and she felt sore.

She stood up and at once, before having to sit back down with ease, it took her a while to notice, but she had been bleeding and noticed the dried, red specks that spread out against her inner thigh and the thin material of her swimsuit. She looked around to see her friend lying a few feet away, with a beer bottle and one shoe lying between them. Claudia crawled to where her friend was lying and used her foot to shake her awake. Her friend groaned and turned over onto her side.

"What happened?" her friend asked,

"Why are your bottoms torn?"

Vita's mother felt a sense of panic, she did not know why her bottoms were torn or why she experienced such intense and radiating pain.

"I don't know. I just woke up, and I have blood, I have blood, and I hurt. I've never felt this before," said Vita's mother.

Her friend, who appeared to still be heavily intoxicated, panicked, "Where have the others gone? Why on earth would they leave us?" she asked.

"I don't know, I know nothing," said Vita's mother before collapsing onto the dirt that was combed over to look like sand.

It was a month and a half later that Vita's mother had learned what really happened, despite her own suspicions, she had up until that point blocked the night from her mind. Her period never came, and it was her mother who had questioned her, questioning the dates of her last period. Her mother was the one who first suspected that her daughter was pregnant.

"Look, you know I don't believe in getting rid of it. Children are a gift from God, and God knows what you did when you were out drinking, but we can't go back now. You said you were with that green boy and his friends."

Her mother never believed that she was assaulted, but rather that her daughter had just given into desire. And maybe she had, at least that is what her mother had led her to believe. Vita's mother focused all her energy on safeguarding her daughter's future, from it being destroyed entirely by the illegitimate child that would surely come.

"You must try to marry and do it quickly. What about one from church? Find one and pray that whoever you pick or whoever picks you doesn't notice, or else you will live a life in poverty and stress, like me." And that is exactly what Vita did. After their discovery, the two of them eyed the boys at the church; watched how they held open doors and kissed their mothers on the cheek.

One week later, during church service instead of closing her eyes in prayer, Vita's mother kept them open, and that is when she saw Vita's father. The only other person in the room with their eyes open, and she knew that if it had to be someone, anyone, it had to be him. He would be the one that would help her conceal her deep, dark secret from all the world. He would be the father to her bastard child. She hoped.

Present day, six in the morning, and more than a decade later, Vita's mother had already cleaned their home and made her family breakfast. An early riser, she much preferred to do the cleaning and prepare meals in silence. Her daughter Vita now stared at her for longer periods of time, as if she were inquiring about her and she was starting to regret that she and her daughter had the conversation over the kitchen sink several weeks prior. Vita was calculative and walked around their large home like a ghost, coming and going, opening, and closing doors she had never opened before. She spent large amounts of time in her father's office. Vita's mother knew there would come a time when she would have to explain to her daughter what happened, and much worse why she had kept it a secret for as long as she had. "I'll wait until she is of age," she bargained to herself.

For only then, she had thought, *would the consequences be a light enough load to handle*. And where would she begin? With her high school graduation? the boy? or her own mother, who at the time back when it all happened, said to her "It would do you well to keep this to yourself and marry a nice boy."

No one questioned her, not even her husband, who trusted his wife with all his human capacities. After sweeping the kitchen floor Vita's mother started a kettle of tea and sat at the family table and fixated on their clean floor. Clean, she liked it when things were clean, cleared of any grime, dirt, and imperfections. The opposite of everything she held within herself, which, according to herself, was messy, and vile.

There at the table, in that moment, is who she was when no one was looking—a solemn faced woman who was grief-stricken, introverted, and bored with the life she had created for appearances alone. Soon enough, when her family would stir, she'd have to put her mask back on and be the woman she had taught herself to be.

VITA

Vita felt faint. Her forehead was clammy, as a sharp pain shot throughout her lower stomach, a pain she chalked up to having not eaten, and as the hunger pains continued, she watched as Grayson's car raced towards her house.

He always sped down her driveway with anxiousness, as if it was something that only her presence could soothe. Finally pulling into the driveway, he sat in his car for a moment, wondering what he should say to the woman who was unlike any other woman he had met. He never knew what to expect. Vita, with a blank stare, watched as he opened his car door, adjusted the collar of his shirt, and headed toward the front porch where she swung.

Vita took a modest sip of brandy, as much as she could stomach; she hated the taste of liquor and only attempted to drink it so that she could calm her nerves. Grayson now looked up at her from the bottom of the stairs. Vita noticed the strings of her shoes had come undone and bent down to tie them. It was the closest they had been since their argument. Hunched over, she said to Grayson, "I am happy you came; I didn't feel comfortable with the way things concluded… you stomping off like that."

Grayson offered Vita a toothy grin hoping she was going to apologize, rush towards him, and ask for his forgiveness. Instead, Vita sat up and smoothed her hands over her thighs, making sure the fabric of her dress had no wrinkles.

It was her body language, the way that she straightened her back and flipped her hair that first showed to Grayson that she would not be apologizing.

"Grayson," she said, "You are a great guy, and any woman would be lucky to have you."

Grayson stood up. His chest puffed out as he stood before her, 6'2, towering over her small frame. She was going to do what he was afraid of.

"You made me drive over just to break things off? I thought you cared, Vita."

"I do care, Grayson, I do. We just want different things, and it took me a while to realize that I was just stringing you along. I can't be the woman you want me to be, nor do I want to be."

She felt as if a weight had been lifted off of her shoulders, she was free the moment the words slid off of her tongue, smooth as silk.

Grayson couldn't contain his frustration.

"I actually came to tell you the same thing," he said, trying to renew his sense of pride and fulfill his ego's desire to be the one breaking up with her.

"See," Vita said, "Deep down, we both know it's what's best."

Grayson, feeling pleased with himself and his ability to recover quickly on the spot said.

"I better get going," and walked towards his vehicle. Despite his tough exterior, Vita saw Grayson as a stray dog, one that would tuck its tail between its hind legs after being kicked away. Vita gave into the urge to curl her lips into a toothless smile of satisfaction. Killing the ego of a man just because she could.

Thinking back to the morning, when she saw her mother sitting at their family's kitchen table miserably. The saddest face Vita had ever seen.

I never want to be that way. Vita thought. Now she could focus her attention on what mattered most to her, her mother's choices, and why she had to make them.

"I made the choices that I felt I needed to make." Her mother's words never left her thoughts. They haunted her and made her question everything. Vita knew that a happy woman never made the choices she *needed* to make but only those choices that she wanted to make.

With Grayson gone, she paced around her father's library, trailing her fingers along the spines of books with titles such as *Invisible Man, The Man Without Qualities*, and

For Whom the Bell Tolls, most of which her dad had urged her to read. It was the foundation of their relationship; his face would light up with pride when he saw her reading and writing. Knowledge connected the two far more than anything else. With her mother, it was different; her mother, who was saintly and polite, always attempting to hold their family together, seemed to always be at a distance from her.

Vita ran her hand across the cool oak and then picked up his fountain pen. On the notepad, which was next to his most recently read book she wrote, "I love you daddy."

VITAS FATHER

He was troubled, he knew something was amiss in his household. A wise man, he had the gift of discernment and had spent many years in speculative silence; as the world around, him prided itself on loudness, he often retreated and observed. Drawing conclusions not on what people spoke of but rather how they carried themselves and their actions. Sitting in his office, he could hear the footsteps of his family, sometimes creeping in and out of closed doors in the middle of the night or long determined strides and paces that quickened with haste.

His daughter, Vita, her steps were wide and long as she rushed to and from classes or paced to match the quickness of her thoughts. His sons were heavy and loud, as they had never been taught to lessen the shock of their presence, the wood floor weakened with each of their steps. His wife's? slow, she walked on the tips of her toes, the perfect example of what it meant to "walk on eggshells."

His wife had become complacent, more complacent than she had previously been. She, with her dull eyes, and sickly disposition (despite her greatest attempts at concealment) had been doing chores and attending events, both present and somehow somewhere else, and he wanted to know where that somewhere else was. The last time he sensed such complacency from his wife was after the birth of their first child, Vita.

He remembered all too well that, from the very beginning of their courtship, Vita's mother hinted at marriage and because he was deeply in love with her, took a knee with a quickness that surprised even himself. They dated for only one month and got married two weeks after his proposal. The two women and his own mother made wedding arrangements, dresses, and invitations with vigor and excitement, and his wife couldn't help but brag about how lucky she was to have found her soulmate so early on in life.

As her belly grew, though, his wife's eagerness and cheerful disposition had deteriorated and, finally, at the sight of their baby, had become serious and solemn. When Vita was three years old, that is when it hit him, though. The truth. Vita's mother was leaning over to tie the child's shoes, the woman's blonde hair shiny in the sun and her pale skin reddened by its rays.

He looked at Vita's mother, then at the child, thought of his own physical features, and knew that his firstborn was not his, and after several weeks of silent observation, he had elected never to speak a word of it or even question the woman who had claimed him as her soulmate. What had been done was done, and his heart had already made a place for the child with brown hair, brown eyes, and a nose so unlike theirs.

DE-DE

De-De peered over her grandmother's body. A new body that didn't belong to her grandmother, at least that is how it seemed. The new one, the one that De-De did not recognize, nor care to acknowledge, was stiff. Grey. It had become apparent to De-De in that moment that spirits, souls, were real things, that they were those which gave the appearance of life itself.

Her grandmother's body lay swollen in the casket with the sort of dullness that only accompanies that which hasn't any real meaning or purpose. *For what good is a house without tenants? What good is a body without a soul?*

The woman's eyes, though closed, were swollen too, her cheeks sunken, and her thin skin, tight with the effects of embalming fluid. Still, it was De-De's turn now. It was De-De's turn to say her goodbyes, to whisper comforting words that would lay her grandmother's body to rest so she'd be welcomed into the pearly gates of heaven. However, De-De stood in silence before the woman's body, and it was hard for her to feel a connection. It felt as if someone had stolen her voice, her talent for finding the right words during times of strife and tribulation, the very voice her grandmother had taught her to use, was now useless. The advocate, for once, was not an advocate, nor did she have the desire to be.

De-De's mother came from behind, placing her bony fingers on her shoulder and squeezing gently to offer comfort. Saved.

"It's okay, baby. It's okay. She knew how you felt."

Her mother said before walking past her, then towards the face of the body. De-De's mother straightened a singular coil that separated itself from the others on her grandmother's head. De-De's mother handled the death well; instead of crying, she doted on how beautiful her dead mother looked and how well the undertaker had done.

And on the outside, so did De-De, appear to be taking it fine, but on the inside De-De was broken, devastated. For her grandmother had always been her comfort in the same way that others find comfort in alcohol, a lover's arm, or a warm blanket. She found comfort in her grandmother's wisdom.

With just one day left before the end of Fall break, De-De wasn't sure how she should move forward or if she even could, but she wanted to be far away. Riddled with guilt, how could she leave her family at a time like that? How could she travel thousands of miles away knowing that the next time she visited home, her grandmother wouldn't be there, with her kind eyes and wisdom offering a recognizable form of solace? She could have asked for an extension from the university, bereavement leave but she didn't want to.

After having one last meal together, De-De's family members gathered in the living room and prepared for their goodbyes. There were a series of "Now don't forget you have a home" and "You make your grandmama proud baby," her little cousins, the ones with plaits and plastic barrettes that hung onto her legs as if they felt that the weight of their bodies would keep her there in the doorway forever, stuck and unable to move forward.

This, to De-De, was the most challenging part, leaving the comfort of familiarity and not feeling any guilt about it. She loved her family, loved them dearly, but each time she stood at the doorway just a few steps away from being back into the world, her inner being leaped with joy.

They did not know, of course, no idea that the De-De they sent away years ago never returned, but instead, a freer version had taken her place. One that knew that she could never reach her full potential staying near her family, who supported her every decision. She kissed her mother on the forehead and brushed her long gray locs, wanting to remember their texture, the feeling of black excellence. At that moment De-De realized most people experience a milder version of death everyday—it occurred in such small ways— nearly undetectable until one day the person realizes that they are different, that things are different, and would never be the same. Her mother hugged her and gave her something small wrapped up in a silk scarf; it was her grandmother's silk scarf. "I want you to have this baby," she said while still hugging her daughter, "but don't open it until you are ready, and you are far away."

This surprised De-De because her mother always yearned for her to stay close, and when De-De elected to go to university several states over, it was her mother who protested in silence with puppy dog eyes and a sullen face.

"I will, mama," said De-De, letting her mother go, and she turned to look at her family one last time before walking to the car that her Uncle Don had already prepared for the trip to the bus station. De-De didn't wait to get onto the bus to open the gift her mother had wrapped in her grandmother's silk scarf; she unraveled it with quickness and anticipation.

There it was, her grandmother's wedding band, the one her grandfather had worked two jobs to buy. It was gold, with a yellow diamond, and two rubies on each side. Yellow diamond for hope, happiness, and two rubies that symbolize family ties. De-De cried. She hadn't cried before then, not even while peering over her grandmother's body, but seeing the ring made her realize her grandmother was indeed gone and would never come back to the earthly planet. She slipped the ring on her thin brown finger and inhaled.

Her Uncle Don sat in the driver's seat, never looking in her direction; some things, like silent grief, didn't have to be acknowledged, and instead, he turned the radio on. De-De took her grandmother's silk scarf and braided it into her hair while "Lean on Me" hummed throughout the vehicle, and the house she had just left grew smaller and smaller until it disappeared.

BENNETTE

He had left August, Dr. Murphy, with her chaos and her erotic book. He adored his wife, more than any other woman he had ever loved, and his affairs were always about commodity and experience until his most recent trip. Never about feelings. But with Summer, it was different.

Something about seeing the way she managed the kitchen, her dark eyes, and how easily she ignored the male gaze attracted him to her. When she laughed, she laughed with her whole body as if he were the funniest man alive, and he liked it. For his wife always kept a part of herself withdrawn, and even in their greatest moments, he sensed that Dr. Murphy wasn't all in. Not in the way that Summer was all in whilst doing even the most basic task, like trying his new recipes or tying her hair up in a ponytail to chop spices. Bennette had begun to develop real feelings for her.

After waking up, like usual, Summer leaned forward, and kissed him on the forehead. She saw the dark shadows beneath his eyes. *He needs sleep.* She thought to herself. They had a few more months in Argentina together, and she found herself experiencing complex emotions—both sadness and exhilaration. Sad because their relationship was coming to an end, exhilaration because she knew that an ending only meant one thing, the beginning of something new. It was all she could do but both soak the experience of Bennette in and accept the fact that she had betrayed another woman, becoming the type of woman she longed despised. *A homewrecker, who leaves nothing but destruction behind.*

A few days later, Bennette picked out flowers. He chose tulips and autumn lilies and watched as the cashier wrapped them in the paper he had chosen. The paper was shiny, its intricate details maroon and forest green, colors that he felt complimented the tulips and autumn lilies the most. Bennette couldn't help but to smile as he thought of Summer.

He'd spent the previous evening shouting out orders over the clattering of utensils and porcelain dishes; all while sharing flirtatious glances with Summer, anticipating the moment they would get to be alone. In his own mind Bennette had imagined a brilliant future, despite his uncertainty, he wanted nothing more than to leave Dr. Murphy and wished more than anything he could be sure of Summer intentions. Bennette noticed Summer would oscillate between lustful giddiness and deep thought, often allowing her mind to drift off amid conversation. He had seen the same shift in most of the women he'd affairs with.

The women weaken beneath the full weight of their choices; being the other woman. They knew Bennette would never leave his wife.

When he opened the door to his small studio apartment, he saw Summer sitting on the bed with her bare back facing him. Her long black hair cascaded over her left shoulder; her skin glistened even in the dimly lit room. He had never seen a more beautiful woman, to him, Summer was even more beautiful than his wife.

"I got you flowers.' He said to her, pleased that he had taken the time to pick them out. The arrangements he ordered for his wife over the phone in the early hours of the morning, were sent with a spirit of obligation, of marital duty, not with any passion, or sentimental value.

Summer turned to face him, her small breast and brown nipples sat high on her chest, they ached for him, and she wanted nothing more than to have Bennette right there, to herself, to feel the heaviness of his body, the thickness of his lust overwhelming her small frame. Her inner thighs were wet the moment he wrapped his arms around her waist and kissed the nape of her neck.

Bennette pushed her forward and pulled her backside up into the air before entering her with an aggressive force. He was a man with needs, and Summer met them all. His body rocking to the sound of the woman's sensual moans and knew without a doubt that he could never go back to his wife. Never.

Across the ocean, in her own home, Dr. Murphy opened all the windows in their loft apartment. She felt happy, the type of girlish dizziness that she hadn't experienced in a long time, and she wanted to hang onto it with everything she had. There was an intense fluttering in her chest as she washed the three dishes that lay in her sink, Dr. Murphy heard the doorbell and soon stood before a delivery man in a brown uniform with a hat that read "Ray's Botanicals." It was apparent that Bennette sent her flowers. While the sentiment was sweet, she couldn't help but feel a slight ping of resentment; she stood at the door staring at them for a good minute before the delivery man cleared his throat, prompting her to respond.

"I am so sorry, they're so lovely; I just had to take them in," she said, with more of a grimace than a smile.

"Yea, they are something," he said and then brought the flowers forward, insisting that Dr. Murphy take them from his hands. She did.

The card attached to the bouquet read "From Bennette, with care and thought, "The Fall Bouquet," *Sweet, and generic*. Dr. Murphy thought, eye-balling the blue hydrangea, certain that the scent was sweeter than Bennette's effort. Dr. Murphy placed the bouquet and its ceramic vase on the dining room table before reaching for the phone to dial Bennette's number. She listened as the phone rang once before going to an automated voicemail that said, "Che Beludo, leave a message." Dr. Murphy did not leave a message; she had simply wanted to give a word of thanks and was relieved to find that he didn't answer that she wouldn't have to pretend that their marriage was okay.

EMMA

When Emma walked into the classroom, each of the four students and Dr. Murphy stared at her, with their lips parted. Emma shaved her head to near baldness, a strong contrast from the thick brown hair she had before Fall Break.

"I love it," said De-De, who sat across the room.

"It suits you," Dr. Murphy said, impressed and restraining the urge to ask Emma why she had done it.

"Thanks," Emma said, with her head down, eyes on the desk before her. The corners of her lips were turned upward, forming a shy girl smile. "You look like Sinead O'Connor, but a better version," said Kat, prompting each of the women laughed.

"So," said Dr. Murphy, "Can I assume everyone had a great break?"

Her eyes went in the direction of Jo, who sat at the desk nearest to her podium; the fluttering in her chest began again, catching herself, quickly adjusting her focus to the others. Then to Bennette.

This is where my focus should be. And though it took her a few seconds, she was able to will herself back into the present moment and present the day's lesson, which would consist of reading "The Yellow Wallpaper" by Charlotte Perkins Gillman.

"Many of you might be familiar with this short story," she said, "It's regarded as American feminist literature. Gillman's piece highlights how women's mental, physical, and emotional health can be disregarded, shrugged off——- treated like a burden."

"I've never read it," said Emma, with her head still lifted, a subtle display of her newfound confidence. "Me either," said De-De. The others nodded in agreement.

"Okay," said Dr. Murphy, "I've printed out copies, please follow my annotations displayed on the projector and make your own while the audio plays." Each of the women got out their pencils, highlighters, and pens and eagerly dove into the text. It warmed Dr. Murphy's heart to see the way each of her students' eyes lit up when they were introduced to a new text. Feeling encouraged that they had somehow created "a room of their own." At the end of class, the five stood in the hallway casually saying their goodbyes. Kat wanted to start a conversation with De-De and had been patiently eyeing the perfect opportunity to do so. It was when she saw De-De's foot pivot forward that her patience peaked, and she couldn't wait any longer.

"De-De!" she called. De-De turned, looked Kat up and down, and took note of Kat's posture, her demeanor, and noticed it had changed.

New boyfriend, I guess, she thought. Kat took timid steps towards her; De-De was the one real friend she ever had. Being completely taken aback by the emotions she felt, Kat collided with De-De and embraced her.

"I am getting help," whispered Kat, clinging to De-De as if she were a life jacket, a good luck charm, something that God had placed on her path for well-being, and she did not want to let go. De-De, who had not yet known how much she needed a hug, squeezed Kat tighter. The crazy, talented, and fragile woman for whom she had originally had no intentions of knowing her outside of the four walls of the classroom.

"I needed a hug," she whispered back to Kat, "My grandmother died."

Emma, who had been watching the two of them from a distance exhaled, she'd been holding her breath. To see Kat and De-De embrace made her think of Ruth. *I need to see her*. Making her way outside she noticed that it had started to rain and stepped from beneath the canopy-covered entrance way to let the rain fall onto her. Emma purposely allowed herself to get drenched. The rain fell onto her shaved head with a coolness that sent a thrilling sensation throughout her body, and she began to walk home.

Once inside her home, she was shocked to see Ruth, her mother, and the church pastor sitting in the living room.

Their facial expressions, a mix of shame and accusation. Ruth looked at Emma, her own face white as a ghost.

"What are you doing here?" Emma asked no one specifically. Prompting Ruth to look down at her shoes.

"Ruth?" Emma said. "Mom?"

"I am so sorry, Emma." Ruth spoke.

Emma's mother, who was on the verge of a nervous breakdown, made Emma feel at once like she was again a child getting scolded in church for sleeping, or scolded for making her two girl dolls kiss. Emma's mother lifted a small woven basket which appeared to hold crumbled pieces of paper and Emma's journal, and Emma immediately knew why they were all there, in that room, looking at her with judgmental eyes.

"Emma, I went into your room to take out the trash and found these letters, these letters to Ruth. I felt compelled to know what was going on, so I read your diary, and this, what you've written about, isn't right, Emma. And now you've shaved your head. You need help, and that is why the Pastor is here; you need healing, and that healing can only come through prayer and the mercy of God."

Emma felt enraged, "Mom, you have no business going through my things, and what I do with my hair is not a question of my sanity or my closeness to God." Emma looked at Ruth, who had tears in her eyes.

"Emma, "Ruth said, "I read the letters, and I, well, I think you misunderstood our friendship, and I don't know what could have made you feel this way about me, but it isn't right."

"Misunderstood?!" Emma shouted.

"Emma, watch your language; who do you think you are? It is not Ruth's fault you are obsessed with her," her mother said, letting out a whimper when the pastor placed his hand on her knee.

"And you mom," Emma said, "trying to act so pure, what about you fucking the deacon? or have you forgotten about your sins? Are you, fucking the pastor now too! Ruth, why don't you tell my mom what you did to me? Where you touched me, where you put your mouth? You are all hypocrites."

Ruth stood up. "I have done nothing wrong and nothing like that with you," she said, she now looked just as angry as Emma's mother. "I agree with your mom that you need help, and I am sorry, but we can no longer be friends."

Ruth flipped her hair, and turned to Emma's mother before saying, "I am sorry; I will pray for you all," before letting herself out of the front door.

Emma took one last glance at her mother and the pastor, who were both speechless. She threw her book bag down and ran up the stairs, before slamming the door and locking it behind her.

VITA

Her time at home during Fall break had proved to be particularly traumatic, leaving her on edge and lacking in security. For no apparent reason, she felt sick, often waking up with migraines and no desire to eat. Much of the week was spent lounging around, nibbling on crackers and the occasional handful of almonds, or toast.

What choices did my mother have to make? And why is father anxious?

"Calm your tits," her brother said to her, pulling her out of a daze. Vita stood near her father's office door as her youngest brother Davy zoomed past her in his rollerblades. Always playing, her younger brother was immature and petulant towards her seriousness, "Calm your tits" was his way of calling her out.

She envied them, the boys in her family. Her playfulness ended a long time ago; it ended when she first realized that her mother treated her differently than her brothers and that her father's expectations of each of the children were differentiated.

Her mother, towards the boys, was warm, sincere, and attentive, but with Vita, she was cold, distant, and looked at her as if they were in direct conflict. It was nearly noon and Vita's father left in the early hours of the morning, expecting him to return soon, Vita had no intentions of leaving her post. She would wait for him and was determined to ask him questions, questions that she knew her mother would not answer.

The night before, for no reason at all, Vita felt drawn to the family photo album. Her eager eyes scanned its sticky pages, for there was something about the photos, something peculiar and off, so much so that Vita did not see herself in any of the faces that were plastered in the photos. There was one photo that made her pause, a family photo, one in which her great-grandmother stood next to her grandmother, her mother, father, and two brothers. Her cousins and aunts. *Why don't I recognize my face?*

Each of them, with their blonde hair, small noses, and blue eyes, looked back at her with a matter-of-fact glance, a connectedness that was so very unfamiliar. Their features were prominent, exact replicas of each of the family members they stood beside. She hadn't inherited the blonde hair, blue eyes, and her nose was large, pointed outwards, defined. Vita wondered where she had gotten her features from. She would wait all night next to her father's office if she had to—to ask questions.

Finally, she heard the hum of misplaced gravel and the low growl of her father's vehicle and straightened her posture, holding the photo album to support the anxiousness that had overtaken her calm demeanor. In a bold and proud manner, she would confront her father, and she wouldn't back down.

— Her mother never entertained Vita's bouts of curiosity, but her father always encouraged her. Surely this time, he will encourage me too.

"Ask questions, Vita, ask until you are content with the answers." He used to say that to her.

When her father opened the front door, it was almost as if he knew that she was waiting on the other side of it with questions he couldn't answer. Once he made it inside, he took off his suit jacket, the one he wore no matter the occasion or time of day and rubbed his balding head.

The man looked tired; his shoulders slouched. A bad meeting? However, when he glanced towards his office door, his demeanor changed. He seemed to perk up and offered Vita a warm smile— To him, it was the only way to appropriately greet his child.

"Vita," he said, the fine lines on his face deepening with his smile.

"Hi, Dad," said Vita, a feeling of warmth washed over her. Her father, always happy to see her, always represented the qualities she admired most.

"Dad," Vita said while touching his arm, "Do you have any pictures of other family members, ones I might not know about? I was looking at these photographs last night, and I……it's silly, but I noticed I am the only one with brown eyes and dark hair. Everyone in our family on your and my mother's side has blonde hair and blue eyes, except for me. I want to know our family history."

Her father's smile disappeared.

"Vita, always with your questions, your curiosity. No one can explain genetics; everyone is all there in that photo album."

Vita, not satisfied with his answer, pushed further, "Yes but …see, everyone knows that if two parents have blue eyes, then the children will also have blue eyes unless, for some strange reason, our distant family members didn't have blue eyes, I don't see how I don't have any of the same features as you and my mom."

Her father looked concerned, nervous even.

"I don't have any information regarding past generations; maybe you should ask your mother." He said it with no incantations and with no care, and this struck Vita as odd.

"But…"

"But nothing, Vita don't worry yourself with frivolous subjects when you are about to graduate from university. Concentrate on your next goal, your plan; that is most important." He walked past her into his office as if she hadn't been standing there, and he shut the door with no hesitation.

VITAS MOTHER

Vita's mother made her way through cobbled webs. It had been far too long since she went through the old boxes that were filled with the elementary art of her children, photo albums, and family heirlooms that had been kept in the attic for the last two decades. She attempted to open the window, both to let in more sunlight and allow fresh air to circulate, her eyes watered in response to the amount of dust on the window. Finally, with a bit more arm strength than she had intended to use, Vita's mother pried the window open and used the leg of an old piece of furniture to hold it open. She peered through the open window, her gaze then focused on her husband's vehicle pulling up the driver.

The woman felt nauseous, she did her best to avoid him and her daughter, for she could no longer endure their inquisitive glances. Her daughter's slow and questioning blink, glossy brown eyes. Her husband's thin bottom lip, which was constantly tucked inside his small mouth. His eyes were sad, giving him the appearance of a destitute puppy.

He was concerned, concerned that she was having another breakdown, like the one she had soon after the birth of Vita. Yet, she was too tired to soothe him, too tired to assure him she was fine, and so the very sight of him caused her to react physically. She had grown tired of trying to mask her moods, her thoughts, which were now too reflective, and even more so, too resentful.

When she heard the front door of her home shut, she turned to open the box nearest to her. It was covered with a thick layer of dust which she brushed off with her slender fingers. Irritated that she and her family had let the attic stay in such condition, irritated that she was the only one that cared. She reached into the box, and pulled out a push pin, then a jar of buttons, feeling around until fingers gripped something hard, like a hunk of wood.

On her tiptoes, she investigated the contents of the box and scanned over the miscellaneous items until she found what she thought she was looking for. A wooden box, one of the high-glossed cherry jewelry boxes that had been so popular when she was a girl. She remembered it to be the box she received on her sixteenth birthday and felt a slight feeling of elation at the thought of having found it. She pulled the jewelry box out of the cardboard one and sat on the floor right beneath the window.

When Vitas mother opened the jewelry box, she closed it immediately and began to question if what she had seen was real. Had she imagined it? *It couldn't be, did you really keep it?* Afraid, she lifted the lid of the jewelry box once again and sighed. She had kept it. A single bottle cap. She acquired it just three days before her wedding. She remembered the moment vividly; how in a fit of rage, on the bank of the lake, she kicked and screamed, rolling in the sand, fisting it, until her body made deep impressions; she was angry.

She was angry with the world and angry at what happened to her. Exhausted, she lay on her back and that is when she turned her head to the left and saw the bottle cap. *It must be the bottle cap from the beer, those beers,* she had thought to herself. It obviously hadn't occurred to her, in the treachery of the moment, that the bottle cap could have come from anyone else's experience, not just her own. Some other high schoolers, who like her glanced out at the water, and hoped for a positive future. That day, the bottle cap, halfway buried in the sand, somehow had solidified her despair. It symbolized her soon-to-be new identity; homemaker, mother to a bastard child, with no real future, and there wasn't anything to hope for.

Vita's mother scooped the bottle cap out of the sand, and pushed it into the pocket of her jeans, physical death, it seemed to her would have been better than having to carry on. That was eighteen years ago, and there she was again, the bottle cap a reminder of who she had become, but this time she knew not to wish for death, for she, for years and years, had already been dead. Vita's mother placed the cap back into the wooden box and gently closed it shut. An unexpected sense of calm washed over her until she heard the footsteps of someone who was walking up the attic stairs.

VITAS FATHER

Though a great deal of time had passed since Vita asked him about the family photographs, his concern regarding his daughter's relentless pursuit of answers plagued him. He knew she would keep pressing and digging until she satisfied her own curiosity. She would ask more questions, which would only lead to the truth, a truth he felt he had no right to tell.

His footsteps were heavy, they acted as anchors that weighed him down, and he had to try especially hard in his efforts to reach the attic. He needed to go through the family photos. He needed to move them to some place that only he'd know about. Finally, at the top of the stairs, he stood at the entrance of the attic, turned the doorknob, and stepped in.

He saw his wife standing near the window, a red bandana tight around her hair, in oversized overalls; she appeared completely undone, and it captivated him. She rarely wore simple clothes or presented herself in a simple manner, and she would never dare to be seen like that outside of their home. He found her beautiful there, just as she appeared before him in her most natural state. A state he so rarely got to see.

"I didn't know you were up here," he said to her, flushing like he used to when they were younger.

"I'm trying to organize everything, clean it out. What are you doing up here?" she asked, her eyebrows furrowed. The two of them stood looking at one another with blank expressions.

Vita's Father had for a second forgotten why he was there; he only focused on the curve of her upper lip, her big blue eyes, almost doll-like. His wife and soulmate. He cleared his throat, "I was going to try and find the box with the family photos," "Vita has a lot of questions, and I was going to take them down to her. She says she wants to know why she has brown eyes." He said it almost like a whisper.

Vita's mother looked down, then back at him. Her shoulders relaxed, and she exhaled. "Well, I don't see why she'd have to look at the photos to know that."

Her husband stood eyeing her, unable to comprehend what she had just said. Did she expect he knew the truth? Did she think he knew the truth all along? They had never spoken about it, never, and now she stood before him, responding in a manner as if he, too, were in on her deep dark secret.

"What do you mean?" He said, partially hoping that she hadn't meant what he knew to be true. That he had made it all up in his head, the reason for their daughters' contrasting appearance.

His wife looked straight through him.

"Well, come on, we both know the truth. I got pregnant, you married me, I had a child that isn't yours." The woman let the words roll off of her tongue, as if she had long been waiting for that exact moment, a moment of reckoning her whole life.

She continued, "I remember the way you used to look at her, then at me, and back again; you knew. I always wondered why you didn't mention it. I waited a very long time for you to expose me, to call me a whore, send me on my way, but you didn't. Why didn't you?" Vitas mother asked.

Vita's father relaxed his shoulders, too; the weight had been lifted. The terribly heavy, suffocating weight, and at once, he realized he had been carrying the burden of pretending all out of fear that his wife had never wanted to marry him in the first place, that it was all a ruse, and that he had passively accepted the truth to spite her. To watch her endure the traumas of secrecy.

BENNETTE

Bennette signed the documents that were sat on his desk by the owner of the restaurant one week prior. The signature actions of a weak man. A man with no gull. The owners of the establishment offered him an indefinite contract with a solid financial offer. "We couldn't have gotten this far without you. and we want you with us," they said to him in a previous meeting.

"Give an amount, and we will give it to you," and Bennette did, an amount he wasn't worth, but to his surprise, they gave him what he requested. All for his personality and reputation, for he knew deep down that any person could do what he did. At that point in his career, most of his service consisted of barking out orders and approving menus, his pawns did most of the work, and they did so in a way that reflected on him positively.

Bennette hadn't spoken to his wife, August, about the offer, as his initial contract was for just six months, and he was to return to the States in just two. There were only two outcomes possible, he had decided, either his wife would relocate to Argentina, or she would stay in the USA. Knowing that their marriage wouldn't be able to withstand the distance, he had deep faith that she would choose to stay in the States. That is when he would ask for a divorce.

He wouldn't have to confront her about his affair nor the end of their marriage; signing the contract did that for him. The contract was his way of making his desire possible. His desire to stay in Argentina, his desire to stay there with Summer. Little did he know, though, Summer didn't want him to stay in Argentina. Summer desired him with an almost primal intensity, viewing him as her conquest. But now that he had succumbed to her seduction, she found herself pulling away, doubting the feelings she once thought were genuine, recognizing that for her, a man like Bennette was good for one thing. The chase.

Later that night, after having already signed the contract, Bennette walked towards the table that sat in the furthest corner of the room. As he made his way toward Summer, he passed several servers who were red in the face, a sweaty, glossy layer of sweat on their foreheads as they carried trays to the loud restaurant. He saw her thin fingers wrapped around the neck of a bottle of red wine as she poured herself a glass. *This Woman.*

Summer didn't know of Bennette's plans, and he looked forward to being able to see her face as he told her the news, to watch as she twirled her long black hair with her finger, her eyes widening in disbelief and excitement. He placed his large hands on the small of her shoulder once he made it to the table, sending a fit of chills down her spine, and she turned to him, looking at him as though she had been surprised to see him. As if she hadn't expected him to show up. This surprised Bennette.

"Hi, look at you," she said, her tone low and husky. There was something different about their exchange, and Bennette felt he was meeting and seeing an aspect of Summer he had yet to see. It was an aspect of Summer that made him feel insecure.

SUMMER

Bennette spent every bit of free time he had in her tiny Argentinian-style house. His visits, once welcomed, had suddenly made her feel smothered. Even his knocks on her door, which she once found to be exciting, were now too loud, too annoying, and disturbed her peace. Now, he stood before her with his usual bouquet; his romantic gestures bored her. It was only a matter of time before her regret would be all-consuming, and she'd no longer be able to stomach the fact that the man's wants and needs had somehow become her responsibility. Summer didn't want responsibility for anything or anyone other than herself, and yet she had somehow seemingly become the basis of a man's happiness when he was only ever supposed to be hers, at least, for a while.

"You look lovely, as usual," he said to her, his brown hair combed over, picture perfect, the way it appeared on his business cards and the posters at the restaurant. "Thank you, you do too," she said in response, stepping away from him, her body out of reach.

"Have you spoken to your wife?" she asked, interested, concerned. Hoping that he had.

"No, it's been a little more than a week. I've been wanting to talk to you about that. About us. I don't want to impose, but I think we both feel the same way. You and me. I've signed my contract; I can stay here with you. Is that still what you want?"

Of course, Summer never said that it was what she wanted; he had imagined her desire to have him long-term and had created a depth to their relationship that never existed.

He appeared to her pathetic, like an earnest child begging for candy or a new toy. His plea was superficial, and it made her feel sorry for him. He reached out to her with his large hands yet again, grabbed at her waist and pulled her closer. The man was handsome. His cologne was rich and romantic, and it made her swoon.

That was the problem; she felt drawn to him when he got close and wanted him. Before long, Bennette, per usual, made his way to her bed after dinner at the restaurant and was already undressing her. It was all she could do but let him, it became routine, a sort of fixation for her, his physical touch.

After tonight, she thought to herself as he laid her back and placed his mouth between her thighs. She moaned. *"After tonight, I will tell him what I really want."*

DR. MURPHY

Dr. Murphy rolled a copy of the New Orleans Review in her hand and tucked it beneath her arm. The New Orleans Review was a big deal, especially for literature professors, readers, and anyone that hoped to someday publish. She'd had her work published in it once, and since then, always warmly accepted a copy whenever one was available to her. Never mind that Loyola University backed it, a different university from her own, it was always an enjoyable read. The issue she had was *Volume 24, Number 2*, with poems by Gallo, Signorelli-Pappas, and a short story by Sheila Mulligan-Web. Six dollars well spent. Six dollars that she very well may have spent on another bottle of wine, which she had recently had too much of on account of everything going on with Bennette.

Finished with grocery shopping, Dr. Murphy made her way to the cash register. There, she met the gaze of a cashier named Molly who had short hair, and a double eyebrow piercing— it glistened beneath the fluorescent lighting, the ugly yellow tint that left an unattractive shadow on the woman's skin–which was thirsty in appearance. With apparent disinterest, Molly rolled her eyes as she scanned items.

"That will be $22.68." she said and Dr. Murphy, who was at first the only person in line, hands began to shake as she forced bills out of her black wallet because a line was forming.

"I'm sorry" she said to the three customers who stood behind her, as if they cared. It was all in her head, their perceived perception of her. Dr. Murphy had a tendency of assuming that everyone in a room was paying attention to her—even though the idea of being the center of attention made her skin crawl. Those were the moments in which she missed Bennette the most, if he were home, he'd be the one handing over money to the cashier, not her.

After handing the cashier the money to pay for her groceries, she decided she would call him and try to amend whatever was broken between them. To add noise to the silence. He'd call her, she'd not answer, and vice versa. Their schedules never seemed to align. She wondered if he'd answer her call as she walked out of the grocery store.

Once at home Dr. Murphy made herself a bowl of ice cream and reached for a book. She flipped through its pages, scanning for a place to begin, and while her desire to contact Bennette dissipated, a desire to contact Jo sprung forth. Of course, she had no reason to contact her, and wouldn't dare. It would be unprofessional.

Instead, Dr. Murphy reached behind herself, took the phone off the receiver, and dialed Bennette's number. It rang once, three times, until there was no answer, and knowing that she tried more than once to reach him, Dr. Murphy relaxed into the comfort of her couch satisfied, still suffocating the yearning, to reach out to her student.

She'd have to wait till the next scheduled class, when the students would dive deep into the essays and poetry of Audre Lorde. Audre Lorde's words from the documentary "A Litany for Survival: The Life and Work of Audre Lorde," ran through Dr. Murphys mind.

"I started out like all of us start out, a coward, afraid; it's not to say I am not afraid now; it is to say whether or not I am afraid, I count less. I value myself; I value myself more than I value my terrors." Her voice, like a God's, would shake them all to their core. That's all that mattered really.

EMMA

Emma's mother now walked about the house in utter silence, a disappointed disposition. It was the type of silence Emma had endured most of her life after disappointing her mother or doing anything as an act of defiance. Emma didn't understand why, but after several days of silence, her mother's coldness would eat away at her, make her recoil into herself and bend at her mother's will despite her own deep desire to go against it.

Emma found herself once again at the last step of their stairway, wanting to do anything to fix what she had broken, to receive even just one quick glance from her mother's beady eyes, which were often squinted and fixed to reveal a look of disgust. Emma knew that this time, she couldn't; she couldn't give in to her childlike needs, the need to have her mother's approval.

Emma walked down the long hallway that led to her mother's room; on her tiptoes, she rehearsed in her mind what she would say and anticipated her mother's indifferent responses with a heaviness that caused an imaginary lump to form in her throat. She knocked on her mother's bedroom door and took a deep breath, waiting for an answer. "Yes, Emma," her mother responded, used to the cycle of anger and grief, ending by coercing Emma into sweeping valid feelings beneath the veil of complacency and acceptance. Her mother's tone was all too familiar.

Emma opened the door to her mother's bedroom and saw a warm and expectant smile. Her mother felt at the core that Emma was there to do as she should, which was to apologize, ask for forgiveness, and agree to repent during the next Sunday service. Yet, Emma stood before her, incapable of producing a smile or any semblance of a truce. The low light of her mother's room illuminated her shaved head,

"Mom, when I graduate, I am moving out."

Her words, though spoken softly, were sharp and sent a pain throughout her mother's chest. "Emma," she said, "you can't just move out; you don't know the first thing about caring for yourself, and you won't have my support if you choose to continue to behave as if you weren't raised the right way. God's way." She continued.

"The plan was and always has been that you stay here, get a job, save money, and make your way into the world. How can I trust you to go out into the world on your own when even here, with the church's guidance, the love of me and your father, you still can't get it together."

"Mother," Emma said, this time with a tone of annoyance, "If I could leave right this moment, I would. I would, but for the sake of school, I have to stay here under this roof. I am leaving the moment I receive my diploma, and you can't stop me. You don't own me."

"I do, Emma" Her mother's warm demeanor changed at once, the tone of her voice angry. "Everything we've done for you, the sacrifices I've made."

"Sacrifices?" Emma yelled, "What sacrifices have you made? Cheating on Father? Confining me to this house? Turning my best friend against me? Being a hypocrite?"

Her mother gasped and placed her hand on her chest, reeling at the audacity of Emma to tell the truth.

"You can leave right now if you want, but don't disrespect me, little girl. You are a disappointment, and for the love of God, I can't save you!" she yelled back at her daughter, shaking.

Emma, red in the face with anger, walked out of her mother's room and slammed the door.

In her bedroom, she grabbed her backpack and her journal and made her way to the front door, where her mother stood, looking at her with the face of a demon.

"Move out of the way," Emma said.

"You aren't going anywhere," her mother said, with her hand on the doorknob, refusing to remove it.

And as if a spirit had overtaken her body, the evil spirit of spite, Emma reached towards her mother's hand and wrist, grabbed it, and twisted. She twisted it so hard that her mother yelped out, crying in pain. Both of their faces were red and contorted, eye to eye. Emma watched as tears fell down her mother's cheek and twisted even harder, relishing the pain she was causing, relishing in the newest version of herself, old Emma was buried long ago. It wasn't until her mother let go of the doorknob and fell back that Emma felt the slightest sympathy.

"You are an evil child," her mother whimpered, now sitting on the floor, her long skirt acting as a prop during her moment of hyper desperation. "Get out," she yelled, but Emma was already halfway out the door.

"You are vile, vile, and I've never been so regretful of you in my life," her mother said.

Emma turned, "Vile? If I am vile, it's because you made me this way; I got it from you," and then shut the door behind her.

Emma began walking down the street with only her backpack, journal, and schoolbooks. She had no place to go, not really, and could only think of one person to go to.

When she ascended the steps to the door, which had been painted red, she grabbed the bronze knocker. No one answered, and a feeling of panic welled up inside of her chest. She decided to try again and again and wrapped so hard the tips of her fingers felt sore.

Ruth had just turned the water off and stepped out of the shower onto the plush bath rug beside the bathtub. Drying her hair with an oversized towel, she heard the knocking on her front door and knew that she had to dress quickly. Her parents, out of town for the last two days, left her to be the only one there at their house, the only one who would be receiving any guests.

I wonder if it's him. Hoping that, for some reason, Tom had randomly showed up to take advantage of her having the house to herself for a time.

Forcing her head of wet hair through the opening of her dress, she didn't put on her undergarments, for she had no plans to go anywhere that day, and if it was Tom, she knew they wouldn't stay on long anyway. As she made her way to the front door, the wrapping continued in an almost aggressive manner. Once she made it to their wide front door, she peered through the peephole just to be cautious and saw Emma's shaved head, her large backpack causing her to stand nearly hunched over.

There was an ache in Ruth's chest, one that she hadn't felt since Emma's mother made her stay to embarrass her. She stood staring at Emma through the peephole, both wanting to open the door and run, hiding away from the guilt she felt for betraying her. Ruth watched up until the very moment that Emma had given up, before opening the door.

"Emma…" she said.

Emma, still shaking with a blotchy face and bloodshot eyes, turned to her, and they quickly embraced, resolving everything between them. They were friends, best friends, and in that moment, not even the embarrassment or betrayal they experienced could keep them apart.

Emma swore to herself that she would never speak to Ruth again after the drama that ensued and believed more than anything that she would follow through on her words. However, the moment she saw Ruth, her heart melted. She had nowhere else to go, not really. Had she gone to the church or to a family member's house, they would have encouraged her to go back home, guilt her, and made her feel inadequate in the eyes of the lord. They would insist that she carry a guilt that she no longer had the strength to carry, one that she knew had only weighed her down and would continue to do so if she didn't refuse to carry it any longer.

There on Ruth's plush green couch, the two of them behaved as they always had and began to plan/prepare for Emma's escape. What would Emma do if she had to return back to her own home? She had never worked for a day in her life, nor had she finished school.

"Maybe you can just go back and apologize, at least until the end of the semester, and then leave?"

"I don't want to apologize," said Emma.

"I know, but my parents would never let you stay here, not after your mom gets a hold of them."

Ruth was right; Emma's mother and father had a certain pull in the town. They had hidden their sins and true selves for so long that everyone treated her parents like idols, always doting on their character and the things that they did for the community. The two of them had a lot to figure out.

DE-DE

De-De had a deep, gut-wrenching, feeling even though everything was going smoothly in her life; and she had no genuine concerns. She reached into the cupboard and reached for the Captain Crunch. It was her favorite cereal and the only thing her roommate wouldn't touch.

"Girl, I've never understood how someone eats Captain Crunch," Her roommate said to her once, and since then, De-De bought it.

It was near the end of the semester and De-De, like the others, was uncertain of what she would do. Which direction she'd steer her life in. Having majored in English there were few proper opportunities besides education, grant writing, or publishing. Education seemed fitting, but there were aspects of a teaching career that she couldn't wrap her head around. The standardized curriculum, the requirement of having to dictate how others think or even what they learn. In fact, Dr. Murphy, despite De-De's expectations, was the only professor or teacher that she had studied under who thought outside the box. Who presented information and assessments with a laissez faire energy. If she had to teach, she'd do so with Dr. Murphy's practices in mind. Dr. Murphy's and Dr. Achebe's.

After engulfing the bowl of Captain Crunch, De-De had a sudden urge to call Kat. She was grateful for the woman, grateful for her insight, her tenacity. After picking up the phone and dialing the number, the feeling in the pit of her stomach grew stronger. The phone rang once, twice, and a third time before Kat picked it up— The feeling at the of De-De's stomach grew stronger.

"Hello?" Kat spoke enthusiastically.

"Hey, girl, I was just calling to see what you are doing; want to hang out?"

"I can't," Kat replied, "I've got another AA meeting!"

"Oh," said De-De, proud of her.

"Unless you want to come?" Kat said.

De-De giggled and then paused before saying, "Sure!"

At the Alcoholics Anonymous Hall, there were only plastic chairs and a sad-looking table that held coffee and doughnuts. Glazed doughnuts. De-De looked over various people, one wearing a tweed suit, an elderly woman with white hair and icy blue eyes, then a man with a rugged beard and scar across his cheek. These were some people Kat sat with not once but up to three times a week. "I go whenever I feel I need extra motivation or to talk," Kat said to her.

It wasn't until the woman with the gray hair and icy eyes talked that De-De understood how AA worked for people like Kat. As she listened to the woman speak, she understood the relevance of seeing the world from another's perspective, of listening to someone vocalize similar traumas.

The woman spoke of the day she found her child floating in her family's backyard pool. "We had it all," said the woman, "we had everything we wanted, and I grew careless. I expected the help to watch her, even when it wasn't there," the woman said, the tip of her long nose bending downwards each time she spoke.

De-De looked at everyone that sat still in the uniform circle, each of their eyes wide and focused on the woman who told the story of her tragedy.

"My kid had grown accustomed to the routine he had with her, the nanny, as she had taken my place, my duties. That day, the nanny had an appointment that she couldn't miss and would be gone the whole night. She had scheduled it with me several weeks prior, but somehow, I forgot. Somehow, I forgot I would have to be a mother for once."

The woman continued, "I went home, I drank. We went to the pool. And then he was dead." The woman's eyes reddened, her face puffy with remorse. My husband is the one who found him. I was asleep while he was drowning. I hadn't put down the bottle since, not until I came here. And sometimes I feel that even these meetings aren't enough."

De-De looked over at Kat, whose eyes were teary and full of compassion.

It was the first time that De-De had seen her cry since the breakdown that she had witnessed during the wellness check earlier in the semester. Kat hadn't had it easy in her life, and her addictions and her depression had left her feeling alienated for far too long— but there in the AA hall there was no alienation.

De-De knew now that the AA meetings were what Kat needed, a community, a group of people who could understand the depth of trauma and of loss. Of the darkness that comes with it. The man with a beard and scar on his cheek offered Kat a tissue, and De-De felt the sinking feeling in the pit of her stomach again.

KAT

Traditionally, towards the end of each semester, the university took part in a statewide writing contest. Those who were interested or enrolled in a creative writing course could submit various types of work ranging from academic essays, short stories, flash fiction, or poetry. While waiting for the elevator, Kat noticed the flier, one that she had never noticed before, it read:

"Write for a prize and accolades!"

It called for students to submit a piece of their writing for judgment. According to the flier, the judging would take place outside of the university, by professors outside of the university. There would be a cash prize given to those who got first and second place, with the work itself published in the local newspaper.

This excited Kat, for she had never submitted her work to any contest or publication, and as she stood before the poster, she felt as if seeing the poster was fate; no one, not even Dr. Murphy, had told her that the competition existed. Kat tore the flier down from the elevator door before walking into Dr. Murphy's classroom.

"Dr. Murphy, do you think it would be appropriate to write about sex trafficking?" Kat asked her at the beginning of class.

"For what?" Dr. Murphy responded.

This prompted Kat to dig into her backpack and pull out the flier.

"This," Kat said, pointing to the flier, "there is a writing competition, and all submissions have to somehow be related to Women's Issues, as broad as that subject is."

Dr. Murphy felt embarrassed; how could she have forgotten to mention the writing competition to The Five? The university's one and only creative writing publication opportunity. She had been too preoccupied with her anxieties about Bennette and the feelings inside her that had been stirring for too long.

"I am so sorry; yes, yes, I think that would be a good fit. I am glad you will submit." She then turned to the others, "It must have slipped my mind, but there is a writing contest, and there are several types of writing that can be submitted: Academic Writing, as in research papers, flash fiction, poetry, and short stories. You must also have a professor represent your work, so if any of you want me to represent you, just let me know."

Each of the five students looked up at Dr. Murphy with lustful eyes, she could see from the look on their faces that they were all tossing around ideas in their mind, but Kat had a large smile plastered on her face, a type of smile that Dr. Murphy had never seen Kat smile before.

"Ya going to submit?" De-De asked Kat as they walked out of class.

"I might," said Kat, "Why? you going to submit?"

"I might," said De-De, letting out a deep chuckle.

"But I think that you should. I've read some of your work, girl, and you've got this sort of style, the type of style that leads a reader on and captivates them. I don't think I've quite mastered that yet."

"Well, now you are just being nice."

"I am not being nice; I think you should do it; you have to; I'll even read it for you before you submit it. Two sets of eyes are better than one!"

De-De knew she wouldn't be submitting any of her own work; she simply didn't have the time and felt that she should spend what little energy she had left encouraging Kat.

Later that night, despite still having several days to write what she'd submit, Kat sat in the middle of her living room floor. Child labor, forced marriages, she thought. She did not know why her mind went to the scenarios or situations or why she felt the desire to write about the immoralities of sexual abuse, but she did. Deep, darker subjects meant to terrorize. Kats black pen glided over the notebook pages smoothly and words formed onto the paper as if the story had been inside of her all along, as if it had been waiting for that very moment to come out. It took her forty- five minutes.

Forty-five minutes to pen a short story that ended up not being about an Indian child forced into marriage. When she was writing, it was as if someone or something had taken over her body, replaced her soul with another being. One that was more confident, and one that had something it needed to say. The title of the story was: Getting Milk. After a moment of contemplation, she lit a cigarette and began to read what had been written:

GETTING MILK

"It was the middle of April. There was no lightning nor any thunder, and the rain that fell seemed to do so in silence. It was that calming mist that we are all so familiar with. The type that incites our desire to sip warm tea and curl up with our favorite book.

Although she could not go outside to play on account of the timid April shower, Krishna didn't mind and spent most of her day making the perfect birthday card for her father. Her mother had kept her busy with the task by giving her a very large container full of construction paper, markers, and other supplies.

Per usual, Krishna's father, a security guard, had already left for his overnight shift at work. When her mom called for her, she quickly put her glue stick down and folded the construction paper in half, making the card complete. She stuffed her feet into her pink rain boots and rushed down the stairs with fierceness, almost crashing into her mom, who stood waiting in the doorway. Their final task of the evening would be to head to the local market Save-a Bit to buy milk, as it was the only ingredient, they were missing to make the birthday cake. Baking a cake for her father had become their small family's tradition.

Her mother asked her to buckle her seat belt before slowly backing out of the driveway. The rain, for the most part, had subsided, and Krishna had played a game of drawing stick figures in the fog of the window. Once inside the store parking lot, where her mother parked the car, Krishna quickly unfastened her seat belt and erased her drawing from the window as her mother reached over to grab her large, oversized purse. Meanwhile, just a few feet away, Jack, a 32-year-old mechanic, had cracked the passenger side window of his 1980s Chevy to let the smoke from his cigar escape.

He took a sip of his Coors Light and, in almost perfect timing, noticed Krishna prancing across the parking lot in her pink boots. He chuckled at her repeated attempts to adjust her large pajama pants. Krishna had caught his attention. Her braids, which rested about an inch from her bottom, and the pink barrette that was fastened beside her left ear. He figured she was 8, maybe 10 if she was naturally small in stature. In observance of her skin complexion, he assumed she was probably of mixed race or Latina, which was especially lucrative, as a mixed-raced or Latina child was frequently requested by his most wealthy clients. He reached into his pocket for his phone and saw the time, which read 7:22 pm. Jack then went to his contacts and clicked on the name Pat. He sent a single text that read,

"Pink boots, pajamas, with mom"

He watched as a woman. Clearly, Krishna's mother placed her hand on the child's shoulder as she guided her toward the entrance of the store. Krishna and her mom went to aisle 7 and started to comb through the many colors of decorative icing.

Krishna was fascinated with the icing that contained edible glitter. "I think daddy would like this one," she said as she held up Gold Glitter icing to her mother's face. "And this!" she exclaimed, lifting a birthday sparkler. Her mom quickly put the two items into the basket and advised Krishna that they needed to go get milk. "I have to go to the bathroom first," Krishna said as she squeezed her skinny legs together. Annoyed at Krishna's sudden need to relieve herself, her mother looked around and saw that the stalls were only an aisle away. The store was, for the most part, empty, and with her parental judgment, decided that Krishna could go by herself. She lifted her hands in the air and signaled to Krishna.

"Hurry up. I'll be getting the milk."

Pat was a nighttime stocker for Save-A-Bit, and most of his evenings consisted of organizing products or replacing price tags. It was an honest living for what it had seemed, and he worked at an admirably steady pace. His pace was a part of the procedure, as he needed to work as if it were his only source of income. He had painted the picture of the perfect employee. His coworkers always referred to him as dedicated.

That he was. Dedicated to Jack and the business they had built.

When he had received Jack's text, he knew he had to shift his focus. He searched for a little girl with pink boots and pajamas. Finally, he saw them. From afar, he anticipated a moment, any moment that would enable him to get the child away from her mother, and just as he was thinking of an excuse to "bump" into them, he saw Krishna energetically skip to the lady's restroom. He texted back to Jack "RESTROOM" Jack took one last sip of his Coors Light, shut off the ignition of his Chevy, and headed inside the store. Pat walked toward the refrigerated section of the market and pretended to scan items like yogurt and cheese, which would ultimately lead to the little girl's mother. When he finally made it next to her, she greeted him with a smile. In silence, he watched the curve of her back as she reached inside the cooler to pull out the milk from the very back.

It was a habit of hers to reach for the product in the back. She always thought the items in the front were less fresh. Pat continued to stare at her and, by instinct, licked his lips as the woman's shirt yielded to her movements and revealed caramel cleavage, her waist, and the braided belt that hugged it. He thought she had a nice body and wondered *if she worked out. When Krishna's mother closed the cooler door, she noticed Pat standing next to her. His stillness was startling. "Excuse me," she said, thinking she was interrupting his pricing. "No, ma'am, excuse me, customers first," he replied while adjusting his name tag. Krishna's mother let out a small giggle and adjusted her bun.*

Pat had to think quickly. "You know, it's not true what they say about us putting the good stuff in the back." Krishna's mother, embarrassed, replied, "Really? Well, thanks for telling me that. Next time, I won't make such an effort." Pat put his scanner down and reached out to take the milk from her, "Here," he said as he attempted to take the carton of milk and accidentally grazed her fingers.

Their hands fumbled over the carton before she gave into Pat's extraordinary customer service.

There was something mysterious and unrelenting about the gentleman that stood before her. It was that moment of awkwardness in which she thought of Krishna at the restroom, and her heart skipped a beat.

Though she was grateful for his attempt to show kindness, the simple act had left her feeling uneasy. She forced a "thank you" to him, quickly pushed her shopping cart forward, and rubbed her neck to relieve the sudden onset of chills. Once she made it to the rest area, she opened the bathroom door and called Krishna's name. Krishna did not answer. She called her name again, a bit louder. Her mother then pushed the buggy inside of the bathroom. Though she saw no feet, she assumed Krishna may be playing a trick on her, so she opened the first stall and said excitedly,

"Got you!" She did this with all seven of the stalls before she confronted the stark truth: Krishna was not in the bathroom. She quickly went back to aisle 7, expecting to find her there, as Krishna was most excited about cake decorations for her father's cake. Aisle 6, 5, 4, 3, 2....she could not find her daughter.

Panic had officially set in. She had never lost Krishna before. Krishna always did as she was told and hurried back when her mom let her go off alone. She left her buggy and ran to the customer service desk, where the cashier's face quickly mimicked her own: a face of desperation.

"Krishna. I need you to call Krishna over the loudspeaker. My daughter went to the restroom and now I can't find her".

The cashier quickly pressed the page button and announced,

"Krishna, please come to the front of the store. Your mother is waiting for you".

The intercom was alarming, but nothing was more alarming than the absence of Krishna's presence.

Little did Krishna's mother know she had been found, found by him. Jack. Several minutes prior to the announcement on the loudspeaker.

"Hi, I like your pants," Jack said to the little girl.

"Hi," she said. "I like your bear. Where did you get him?"

"Well, if you like this one, I can give it to you. I have another one in my car, just like this one, except he has a red bowtie".

"Really?" Krishna got excited and started to think of a name for the bear.

"Do you think you could go get it and bring it to me? I have to go find my mom." Jack started squeezing the bear, and he knew he was running out of time. "How about we surprise her? We can get a bear for her too".

Krishna thought about it for a second and looked at Jack. She saw kindness in his eyes and grabbed his hand.

Relieved, Jack said to her, "Tell me about yourself."

Krishna obliged as she walked through the sliding doors with Jack. "I like candy and playing with my stuffed animals. I even have names for all of them, and they sleep with me every night. Tonight, we are baking a cake for my *dad, and I will decorate it. He will be 46; he already has gray hair and tells me I am the reason that he has it. My mom should be coming to look for me soon, and when she does, she can show you what I picked out."*

Jack held her hand a little tighter."

Kat, after reading what she or *it* had written, got excited. She jumped up and down in her living room, and her children soon appeared behind her. Turning to them, she grabbed their tiny hands, and the three of them spun in circles with a giddiness they hadn't experienced in quite some time.

Their mother was happy and excited but, most importantly, alive. It was just a small writing contest, and Kat knew that, but somehow her participation in the competition gave her more proof that she really was going to be okay. She and her two children. It solidified to her that she was beating the darkness and not just managing it.

VITA

The family's marble water fountain glistened beneath the yellow sun, creating a sense of enchantment as Vita sipped her coffee, black, like her father had taken his. Vita attempted to rid herself of a tiredness that had been with her for weeks. A sort of fatigue that she couldn't shake.

She hadn't been able to sleep well, either, not since finding her family's photos and questioning her father about them. He was hiding something, and all she wanted to do was find out what.

If I drink another cup, I'll get sick, she thought before hearing the low creak of the screen door. The sound distracted her from the nausea that she felt, and she turned to see both her mother and father standing there with their own cups of coffee. The two of them, picture perfect, even in the early morning with bed hair and robes, eyed her as if she were a wild fawn. *Something's amiss.* Almost intuitively, Vita slid over to the furthest side of the swing and made room for the two of them. She tapped the side of her coffee mug as they made their way to the porch swing; it buckled at their weight, causing the swing to sway.

Her mother was the first to make a sound, a sigh, and Vita couldn't tell if it was a sigh of relief or a sigh of exasperation. Her father whistled, that same whistle he had done since she was a child. It was a sound that she would listen for when she'd stay up waiting for him to come home from work.

The three of them swung in silence.

"Vita, we have something that we would like to talk to you about," her mother said, finally breaking the silence.

Naturally, her mother looked out towards the yard rather than looking at her. It had become common for her mother not to make eye contact.

Vita instinctively knew where the conversation was headed.

"Is it about the photo album?" she asked, not wanting to waste any time.

"It is," her father chimed in.

Her mother continued, "I blacked out one night at the lake."

The three of them sat in silence after her mother's statement, with only the rhythmic rocking of the porch swing offering a response.

"And?" Vita replied. In an unexpectedly haughty tone.

"And, because of that situation, that experience, I got pregnant. I got pregnant with you."

Vita's mother continued, "When I found out that I was pregnant, it devastated me; I couldn't believe that the person who had done that to me had also given me something to remember him by, as if the brutal rape wasn't enough. And my mother, your grandma, knowing that I had ruined my future ...Well, she took control of the situation. She came up with a plan, and I went through with it."

Vita felt a sudden surge of irritation, "And what plan was that?"

"Well, I needed to marry." her mother said in a matter-of-fact tone.

"So, you," Vita said, "you, what? You got with my father, well, he's not my father, is he? You got with him to hide the fact that you had a bastard child?"

Everything had made sense to Vita now. Her mother saying that she "did what she had to do," her emotional distance, coldness, and general unhappiness. Her mother built a life that masked the truth, but all it did was alienate Vita and cause her to dissociate.

"It wasn't like that, Vita," her father chimed in.

"And you," she continued, "did you know all along, or has she been lying to you too? I asked why I look so different, and you told me…you made me feel as if I were being dramatic!"

"Honey don't take it out on your father, he…" her mother spoke until Vita interrupted her.

"Well… did you know?" Vita looked at her father. His blue eyes seemed to absorb the morning light, matching the blue sky above.

"I always suspected, honey. And that is the truth. I just loved you and your mother so much that it never even crossed my mind to do anything other than accept it." Her father's response was genuine; genuine just like he'd always been.

"My brothers…. do they know?" Vita asked.

"No," her mother said and reached for Vita's hand, to which Vita refused.

"But we should tell them, I suppose."

The three of them swung in silence once more.

Early the next morning, Vita made her way to the University. There was that pain again, a sharp, dull ache that felt like a pinch at the left of her stomach. She shrugged it off as usual, as it had become a habitual inconvenience, and made her way around the circular table at the center of the counselor's office.

With everything being out in the open, her mother's past, the reason behind her own facial features, and the truth, Vita wanted nothing more than to focus on her life after graduation. Manipulated by Vita's grandmother, Vita's mother spent her whole life beneath the weight of secrets, lies, and guilt, and Vita wanted nothing more than to get away.

Knowing what happened to her mother incited a deep yearning in Vita; she yearned to do as she pleased, just like her mother wanted for herself twenty years prior. Vita wanted to focus on education and learning, to exist only for herself. To be selfish. As she made her way through the counselor's file cabinet, the one with blank college applications and pamphlets, she stumbled upon one for The Iowa's Writers Workshop in Iowa City, Iowa. Vita did not know which college interested her the most, but she knew that she wanted to be surrounded by creativity and wanted to focus on literature and writing.

According to the pamphlet, Iowa's Writer's Workshop was a two-year residency program that would lead to a completed thesis of either a novel, short story, or collection of poetry and a Master of Fine Arts. The acceptance rate was extremely low, and the program itself was highly competitive. While "the best of the best" is subjective, Vita knew that a student's admittance into that program meant they were themselves "the best of the best." Before shutting the filing cabinet, Vita grabbed three applications. One to Smith College, the Iowa's Writers Workshop, and NYU. She located the empty business folders stacked neatly in an empty basket, three of them, along with pens and paper clips.

She would spend the next few days, weeks, filling out the applications and typing her essays on the Commodore 6000 Word processor that her father had purchased from Radio Shack several months prior. It would take at least two weeks for her to receive admittance letters, if she received any at all, and she would wait, patiently, because they'd determine a part of her path.

After gently shoving the applications and supplies into her tote bag, Vita made her way to Dr. Murphy's class but was shocked to find a handwritten letter taped to it. The note stated that class had been canceled. The others arrived soon after and were just as disappointed. It was the first time that Dr. Murphy had not been in attendance, and it was the first time that each of them arrived at class at the same time.

"Well, I guess we have a free day," said Kat, to which De-De replied, "You always have free days" and laughed. It was true Kat had missed more classes than the other students, and it wasn't until recently that she was attending both classes each week.

"What should we do? Catch up on our assignments?" Vita said, "I could use the time to fill out more applications."

Emma, who was still staying at Ruth's house, chimed in, "To be honest, I am going to take this day as a personal day" Her hair was growing back, and she had developed a habit of scratching her scalp whenever she was anxious.

"Maybe we can go walking around the French Quarter?" Jo suggested.

"The French Quarter?" said Kat, "What is there to do there in the middle of the day?"

"I don't know."

The five of them made their way outside, where they were blasted by the sunlight. De-De and Kat walked beside one another.

"Have you started your short story?" De-De asked and was met with a wide grin from Kat. It was toothy and full of vitality, and De-De knew that Kat had.

"I finished it," she exclaimed. "And I think it might be good."

"Really?! that's so great."

"'What about you," Kat said, "Have you started yours?"

"Yes, of course I have. Yours might be good girl, but mine is great. I'm going to win!" De-De said, teasing Kat. She hadn't started her own short story, nor did she intend to. She wanted to encourage Kat, and she wanted Kat to feel as if she had even more competition than she had.

"Ha," said Kat, "We will see; I am pretty sure my story will get first place. I wrote it in under an hour." The two women chuckled at one another and kept looking forward, following behind the other three, who were just a few steps ahead.

When they made it to the parking lot, Vita lifted an open hand to her forehead to shield her face from the sun.

"So, what is it? hangout or do our own thing."

"We could all go get tattoos," Jo blurted out.

"You with your ideas." said Kat, shielding her face from the sun, too.

"Well, actually, I'd do it." said Emma.

"Me, too."

"Me, too"

Kat sighed, "We get a little bit of free time, and everyone wants to permanently mark up their bodies."

"Well, think about it, when will all five of us be in a class together again? A class like this? Jo replied.

"You, you're going to go off to grad school, right? De-De too, likely. Emma…"

"I'm leaving right after graduation," Emma said, finishing Jo's sentence for her.

Jo continued, "And Kat, Kat she's creating a whole new life for herself."

Kat smiled.

"And as for myself, who knows, but I feel really good about it." Jo replied, genuinely not sure of the direction she would be taking after graduation.

Vita chuckled. She hadn't told anyone in the group what had been going on in her life, and there in the parking lot discussing the prospect of getting a tattoo, she felt the need to tell someone, anybody.

"Yea, I just found out that my dad isn't my dad; how's that for change." She said, looking towards the ground.

"My mom kicked me out," Emma said to fill the silence and smiled.

"Oh, no," said De-De before saying, "Well, my grandma died."

Kat reached out and caressed De-De's shoulder.

"I… I am in AA, broke up with my boyfriend, have crippling student debt— at 27 years old," she said.

"See, yea, my dad, who I haven't seen since I was 7!" Exclaimed Jo "showed up at my apartment, asked me for money, and never came back. I already knew he would not come back. By the way Kat, I am 32—I've got you beat."

"I want to do it," Vita said, "Let's do it."

"But what would we get?" Emma asked. "Are we going to get matching ones?"

The five of them stood thinking for a moment before De-De spoke.

"We delight in the beauty of the butterfly but rarely admit the changes it has gone through to achieve that beauty."

"That's Maya Angelou," said Kat.

"Yes"

"We should get butterflies!"

"Exactly," said De-Dee

Emma agreed. "We should get butterflies! Blue butterflies—they can symbolize having peace and faith in our life. Past, Present, and Future."

"It's settled; we are going to go get tattoos!" Jo said, already having several of her own.

The tattoo parlor they went to appeared to be sketchy. It was the fluorescent lighting, the smell of mildew, and the cracked window that made it appear so.

"SHADOW INK," it was called, and a man named Little Pete made the place appear even sketchier. It was the third tattoo parlor they had visited on account of Jo not having a valid form of identification; Little Pete was the only one who would accept them as an entire group and the only one that would allow her to get one, too. Jo looked extremely young for her age.

"What happened to Aart Accent?" whispered De-De to Jo.

"I called, Miss Jacci wasn't there, and they said I couldn't go in without my ID without her being there."

"I thought you knew them real, real, well?"

"Me too," said Jo, shrugging her shoulders.

On the walls of the small room, there were outlines of tattoos, both big and small, on sheets of thick paper. There were Friday the 13th tattoos, roses with thorns, dolphins, and cartoon characters. The art sheets were covered with a thick clear plastic that glistened beneath the parlor lights.

"What are y'all thinking of getting?" Little Pete said, adjusting his pants in the vilest way. Little Pete had shaved his head clean and adorned it with tribal designs. It was strange that his name was Little Pete, for he was a large man, barely able to fit into the chair that he had hastily pushed towards the front desk.

"Maybe we should go somewhere else?" De-De whispered into Kats' ear, "We could catch hepatitis."

"No," she whispered back, "I'm too committed now."

"We want butterflies," Jo said, "Do you have any drawings of those specifically?"

Little Pete grunted before reaching beneath the glass desk and grabbed a thick photo album. He turned the pages before stopping and using his fat index finger to point to the one butterfly design on the page. It was small. A dainty little butterfly with thick lines.

Each of them leaned over to look at the design that they would have on them for the rest of their lives, a silly grin on their faces. This annoyed Little Pete, so he rolled his eyes.

"Where do you want it?" he asked, and then "'who's first?"

"I want to go first," said Vita, surprising the others, "and I want it here," she said, pointing to the inner side of her arm, the area between her wrist and shoulder bone.

"Right there?" Jo asked.

"Yea, that's where I want it," Vita said, looking at Little Pete. "And I want it to be blue."

Little Pete lit up a cigarette before standing and said, "Alright, let's get this over with. Head over there to that chair while I set up."

They watched as Little Pete walked towards the back of the shop, his large body jiggling in waves.

One by one, they got their tattoos.

Jo got hers on her left foot and De-De, behind her ear. Emma, on the nape of her neck, knowing it would get covered by the recent growth of her hair should she choose to let it grow out. And Kat, Kat got hers on her right shoulder.

DR. MURPHY

The woman behind the counter stared back at Dr. Murphy with dark eyes. Her thin eyebrows were furrowed as she searched the system for flights to Argentina. Dr. Murphy had chosen to fly to Argentina on a whim and had not thought about the complexities of scheduling. She went into the airport determined to give Bennette a surprise visit, carrying with her only one suitcase and the book that Jo suggested to her. She notified the dean that she would be taking time off, missing both her Tuesday and Wednesday classes of the following week.

That would leave her six days. As the woman before her leaned in closer to the screen and scrolled through the open seats on upcoming flights, Dr. Murphy scanned the airport lobby. Nearly full, on a Thursday night, people pulled luggage behind them, pushed children in strollers, and waited for their suitcases to make their way around the conveyor belt.

"I have one seat available; it leaves tomorrow morning at 5:00a.m; there was just a cancellation." The woman said to her, "How will you be paying for the flight itself? Cash? Card? Economy? First?"

"Economy and card" she would use her own credit card, the one that she didn't share with Bennette. The one that she only ever used for miscellaneous occasions, like a random flight to Argentina. Dr. Murphy didn't want to wait till the end of his contract to figure out what that something was, especially because she had been flirting with the possibility of leaving her current position at the university, for another.

Despite the apparent disconnect between her and Bennette, she thought maybe she would encourage him to extend his contract in Argentina and move to be near him, or perhaps, he would move on to some other place, and she'd travel along. These were all hypothetical scenarios that she had imagined justifying her need for change, to leave the university, and while she wasn't happy with Bennette, she couldn't imagine not having him at her side.

It was something all marriages went through; she had supposed, a rough patch, a season of complacency, *where habit is the only thing binding us*, she had often thought.

Knowing that her flight wasn't until the next morning, Dr. Murphy purchased a one-night stay at the nearest hotel room. It was a tawdry place that smelled of cigarette smoke and mold, but she didn't mind it; she was raised to be frugal, and well, she could hardly see spending more than what she had for just six hours of sleep.

All she really needed was a hot shower, a shot of whatever alcohol the hotel carried, and a place to sit; she likely wouldn't even pull the blankets back on the bed. At about 3:00a.m. in the morning, Dr. Murphy stood up, straightened her clothes, and double-checked her flight information. She needed to be at the airport at least two hours earlier, and after gathering her belongings, she shut the door behind her and made her way to her vehicle.

The flight was bearable enough. With the metaphorical calmness that comes before a storm, Dr. Murphy effortlessly imagined the interaction she would have with Bennette. She imagined his tall stature, his round puppy dog eyes, and the look of surprise that might take over his usually neutral face when she'd finally be standing before him. It was an eleven-hour flight, non-stop, and it would be 5:00p.m. when she'd finally exit the airport and step foot on Argentinian land.

Buenos Aires, Argentina, the touristy city that Bennette had lived in for nearly six months, captivated her. There were buildings and houses painted in colors of deep pastel, neon blues and oranges. Cemeteries with extravagant mausoleums and street vendors with flowers such as Ceibo and Autumn lilies– fruits like prickly pears and Chilean Myrtle, too. She hated to admit it, but it was romantic, the atmosphere bled romance, and she could see how two strangers could meet and fall in love in a city such as that. How Bennette might fall for a woman named Summer, there.

The taxi driver, a man with dark skin, smooth like expensive leather, got out of the vehicle and held the door open for her. He then went to the back of the vehicle, where he lifted the door to the trunk and assisted her with her luggage; offering an enormous smile of satisfaction, he pointed to the entrance of the hotel. Dr. Murphy stood before the man for a moment before realizing that he was asking her if she needed further help and signaled to him, she could manage her luggage on her own.

The man nodded, shut the trunk of the car, and made his way back to the driver's seat. Dr. Murphy inside of the hotel, her feet sweating in her off-white sneakers, switched her luggage from her right hand to her left.

She was met by a pretty woman with silky black hair and hazel eyes. "Buenos Tardes," the woman said with a warm smile and reached out her hands to Dr. Murphy; this was the polite way to greet someone, Dr. Murphy remembered and reached out to take the woman's hand in her own.

"I. Only. Speak. English," Dr. Murphy said to the woman, embarrassed.

"Ah, it's okay, I. Speak. English. too," said the woman, with a very clear English accent.

"Most of our visitors don't speak Spanish" the woman continued, "How can I help you?"

"I have a room here, under Murphy."

"Okay," said the woman, "Let's see if we can find you. Do you have your Driver's License?"

"Yes," said Dr. Murphy.

"OH! Another Murphy!" the woman exclaimed.

"No, this is my first visit."

"Really?"

"Yes"

The woman's facial expression changed. Her eyebrows grew closer together as she looked at the computer before her.

"Well, I guess Murphy is a popular last name."

"Is there another Murphy in the system?" Dr. Murphy asked, curious.

"Yep, says so right here. I always find these sorts of things funny," said the woman before reaching into the drawer nearby. Dr. Murphy wanted to ask her about the details regarding the other Murphy in the system.

When was the other reservation made? She wanted to ask, but instead just stood there, saying nothing.

"Okay, you are all set, Mrs. Murphy; I hope you enjoy your stay."

Dr. Murphy grabbed the room key from the woman, "You too," she said before adjusting her luggage and pulling it towards the elevator that was nearby.

In the room, the first thing she did was try to open the antique bay window, the type that only allowed for the outer windows to open, the center one fixed. The sunset, covered by cream-colored clouds, hid beneath the city's eclectic houses, and gilded the many strangers that crowded the city's busy streets with a romantic golden hue.

Dr. Murphy planned to wait till the following day to reach out to Bennette, and not any sooner. She would get dressed and find her way to the restaurant and appear to him as a guest waiting to be served.

After a hot shower, the next day, Dr. Murphy made her way into the streets of Buenos Aires with the tourist guide, a thick booklet offered to guests as a gift of gratitude for their stay, from the hotel. She flipped through the pages of the booklet only half interested because she was only truly visiting Buenos Aires for Bennett, and as far as she was concerned, it was all that mattered. Referring to the street map at the back of the travel guide, Dr. Murphy identified she was on Avenida Corrientes, about four blocks from where she needed to be, the new restaurant, Sabor Alimentos, in which Bennette was the main chef.

Around noon, the air of Buenos Aires was fragrant, almost like a sweet floral perfume mixed with spices like tobacco and cinnamon, and people passed Dr. Murphy by with quickness, for they had places to go, and she, with her map, was slowing them down. After several mishaps, like taking the wrong turns, she arrived at the restaurant and pushed her way through the heavy glass doors thirty minutes past noon and sighed as the cool air hit her sweaty face. A tall woman who appeared to be no more than eighteen greeted Dr. Murphy with a smile soon after. Dr. Murphy read the woman's name tag.

"Mariposa," it read.

"I'd like a table, please, somewhere near the back," said Dr. Murphy, straightening her linen dress, smoothing out the wrinkles from the walk. It was green and loose fitting. Braless, the thin material rubbed against her breast anytime she moved. Her blazer offered her a bit of coverage, though.

"I have the perfect place," Mariposa said. "Do you like music?" She asked.

"Yes, Yes I do," Dr. Murphy responded.

"Okay, I'll sit you right next to the guitarist! Come," Mariposa signaled Dr. Murphy.

When Dr. Murphy sat at the table, the server handed her the menu, and she let her eyes linger over the whole of it. The food, drinks, and desserts that were listed and pictured were all the product of Bennette, his creativity, his greatness, and he made it easy for her to imagine how each of the dishes might taste. For just a moment, Dr. Murphy felt proud to be his wife. She saw right at the top of the dessert menu, "Helado de chocolate con menta, chocolate ice-cream with fresh mint and whipped cream," and knew that Bennette had been thinking of her when he created it.

She decided that she would take her time eating. After sipping the most expensive wine and enjoying the sweetest dessert, she would make her request. A request to see the chef.

First, she had a fried empanada for an appetizer. Then she ordered Argentine Sea fish---a white fish grilled and doused in chimichurri, a sauce made of garlic, olive oil, chili, oregano, and vinegar. Steaming the vegetables, the chef placed them right beside the meat, creating a presentation worthy of a portrait. Last, she had dulce de leche, a creamy dessert that melted in her mouth. This was all, of course, washed down with a Cantina Zapata Malbec.

The server came to her to offer water and cleared the table. "You didn't like it?" he asked, looking down at her half-eaten meal, "Ah yes," she said and rubbed her belly, "It was amazing." He asked if she needed anything else, and Dr. Murphy, after already having three glasses of wine, took him up on the offer.

"Yes, I'll have water," she said, and then "Could you also ask the chef to come out? I want to thank him for this meal?"

Music from the guitar intensified the mood.

"Yes," said the server, "Anything else for you, ma'am? What about the check?"

"Yes, please bring the check."

Dr. Murphy poured one more glass of wine from the bottle of wine that she had nearly finished. She didn't know why, but there was something about the server's facial expression that made her nervous and second-guess her decision to surprise her husband. Her confidence recoiled. It was when she took the very last swallow of her wine and then felt the very first effects of intoxication that she also felt a tap on her right shoulder.

It was a gentle tap, one that felt unfamiliar. She looked up, and her eyes met the face of a woman, a woman with what appeared to be dark hair tucked beneath a white toque and knew that it was Summer. She could gather that just from the information that she had received from Bennett over the course of the last six months.

Tall, whimsical, his type, for sure. Still, Dr. Murphy had only assumed that Bennette was having an affair; she had no proof, and so she sat looking up at the woman that she had imagined and forced a smile. The two women stared at each other before Dr. Murphy broke the silence.

"Hi," she said through a clenched jaw. "I wanted to meet with the chef, I am his..."

"Wife?" asked Summer, with a warm and endearing smile.

"Yes. You must be Summer?" Dr. Murphy replied.

"Yes," she said, eyes deadlocked on Dr. Murphy's face.

"He just went to the market to get a few supplies. Our shipment hasn't come in."

Her eyes shifted focus, and she scanned the room. After removing the torque, revealing a tight bun at the top of her head, her gaze met the eyes of Dr. Murphy once again.

"I wanted to surprise him; he doesn't know I am here. How long do you think he'll be?"

Dr. Murphy asked.

"Not long, maybe an hour? If not less. You should wait. What are you drinking? Summer asked, already knowing the answer because she took inventory of the restaurant's wines and knew each time a customer ordered the most expensive one.

"Cantina Zapata" Dr. Murphy said.

"Malbec?"

"Yes"

The two women were cordial, and Dr. Murphy sensed Summer was trying to please her, to impress her even. The schoolgirl tones that woman had on the phone when she answered the phone in Bennette's was gone and had somehow evolved. It was more mature, less superficial. Likewise, the sight of the woman she had once envied but now pitied surprised Summer, Dr. Murphy was both the plainest, and prettiest woman she'd ever seen.

After leaving Dr. Murphy at the table, Summer went into the kitchen and poured herself her own glass of wine, and quickly gulped it down. Knowing what Bennette had done, and his intentions with the contract, she couldn't help but wonder how he would react when he saw that the woman, he was so determined to leave had come to him to meet with him at a place he used to create such distance.

Does he even know she is here? Summer, too, wondered if Dr. Murphy knew if knew about the affair, and if Bennette already spoke to her about the contract. Either way, to Summer, to see Dr. Murphy was a relief; it meant that she herself wouldn't be Bennette's primary focus, and for the first time in four months, she wouldn't be the object of his desire and affection.

When Bennette walked in, he immediately noticed her. Her side profile, and long brown hair, was something he'd spot in any crowd of any size; his wife carried a certain aura, a sultry and alluring aesthetic. *What is she doing here?* He grimaced as he watched Summer, his lover, walk over to his wife's table.

Scratching the back of his neck with his one free hand, he made his way to the kitchen of the restaurant, put down the sacks, and headed towards the table that his wife was occupying. When he walked up, Summer turned and gave him a cunning smile, a smile she had only ever reserved for him during sex, and then placed her hand on his wife's shoulder. This angered Bennette, he didn't know what sort of game Summer was playing, but he could tell from the two women's demeanor that they had already introduced themselves and knew who each other were.

He met the eyes of Dr. Murphy, whose eyes were low with drunkenness. *She had too much to drink.*

"Bennette!" She exclaimed. "I've been waiting for you; Summer has been taking great care of me." Bennette stood before her, unable to discern if her reaction was genuine or a hint to him, she knew about the affair. He forced a smile as he reached out to her, encouraging her to stand and embrace. He took her in his arms and felt comforted, the type of comfort that came with familiarity, assurance, and it was her that released his embrace, rather than him. He placed his hands around her waist and pulled her closer and let his hand graze over her bottom while looking at Summer.

"Stop," Dr. Murphy said, uncomfortable with such a public display of intimacy. He knew what type of touches got her aroused, what type of touches made her put her guard down.

His grabbing her as if there hadn't been weeks of silence between them seemed like a sort of betrayal and an offensive act.

"I can't believe you're here, that you came all this way for me. What about work?" He said to her, curious how she got the time off to take an international flight.

"Well, I just took the time off. I didn't give them a choice," she answered. It was true. She had hardly used any of the twenty-four days she was allowed per year. Seeing Bennette was something that had to be done; they needed to talk, face to face, whether he realized it.

"Where are you staying?" he asked.

"I am staying at the hotel about four blocks away; what's it called? …. ummmm" she couldn't think of its name.

"El Pedregal?" Summer said, briefly meeting the eyes of Bennette.

"Yes, that's it," said Dr. Murphy, she continued, "It's funny; the woman that booked me in told me she saw another Murphy in the system. Things like that really make me realize how small the world really is. How common names are."

It wasn't that the name was common but rather that they booked a room there early in their affair. And there was something about Dr. Murphy's tone that signified that she knew too.

"Yea, very common," said Bennette. "What's your room number?"

"281." she said.

"I have an idea; how about we go out tonight," said Summer.

Bennette chuckled, "No, no, my wife just got here in this grand city, and I want her all to myself. I'll meet you at your hotel, say, in about an hour. Maybe two?" He said to Dr. Murphy, ignoring the gaze of Summer.

"Sure," she said, "I'll make my way over there now."

"Give me a minute, I'll get you a ride, " Bennette told her, and waved to someone in the distance. The man he flagged down quickly came to his side and the two of them spoke in Spanish briefly.

"All good, he's going to have a ride ready for you," Bennette said, pleased to appear in charge.

Dr. Murphy took two steps forward and reached out to Summer, prompting her to shake her hand, and Summer obliged.

"It was very nice to meet you, Summer; you're a beautiful young woman."

This made Summer smile; she had never before blushed at the complement of a woman, especially not one whose husband she had slept with. It was strange. For a moment, she couldn't help but feel that Dr. Murphy was flirting with her.

"It was very nice to meet you too, Dr. Murphy," Summer said, her cheeks hot.

They held each other's gaze, and Bennette grew uncomfortable.

"Well, better get going," said Dr. Murphy, walking away, turned one last time to glance in Bennette and Summer's direction. *They really would make a beautiful couple,* she thought. Feeling a little too light on her feet, she was grateful to have a ride.

Bennette quickly grabbed Summer's arm and led her to the freezer of the kitchen once Dr. Murphy was out of sight.

"What the fuck are you pulling?" he asked her, close enough to kiss her.

"You could have stayed in the back until I got back. I walk in and see you smiling and laughing with the woman whose heart I am going to break," he said.

"I'm not pulling anything," Summer said, "I was trying to be nice, trying to give you time to tell her the truth."

"Give me time?" Bennette took a step back, he didn't know the woman that was standing before him, nor did he, it seemed, know the newest version of his wife, the one who had booked a flight to Argentina and seemed to flirt with a woman, his woman, right in front of him.

"I'm going to tell her; I'm going to tell her tonight," he said.

"You should, she's a lovely woman. You should tell her your plans."

"You mean our plans?" he responded.

"Bennette, you made plans without me...I never said I wanted you to make those choices." This was Summer's moment, and it came when she least expected it. There was something peculiar about the way Dr. Murphy carried and it made Summer ashamed of what she and Bennette had done. Disgusted that Bennette would do such a thing to a woman like Dr. Murphy.

"You've been involved with me, both feet in, until today, you meet my wife one time, and you forget what kind of person we both are." He spoke.

"I haven't forgotten," Summer responded, "I am tired of my shit, too."

KAT

She stood on her tippy toes, tying the rope around the bulk of the iron that supported the ceiling fan. Satisfied, she stepped down to eye the space between the stool and the entire length of the rope and watched as it swayed. It was a dark and twisted thing to do, but it made sense to her. It made sense to her to confront it. Kat still struggled with depression the melancholia, but she had made great strides since attending AA meetings. In fact, whenever she felt a moment of anxiousness or a bout of existential crisis, she attended AA, sometimes twice or four times in one week. Sitting around the others, listening to their stories, their faults, and admittance to addiction somehow helped her.

It helped her to witness humanity from another perspective, a perspective which she had not often been afforded. Knowing that she wasn't *the only one* made her feel as if she had a chance; her experience was one that was shared.

And now, staring at the rope, the muddy brown color of the wooden stool, she recognized how far she had come and how near to death she once really was. Soon after, she heard a knock on her front door, and as she expected it to be, it was De-De. De-De, who had been struggling with the death of her grandmother found comfort in being in Kats presence. Kat was delighted, proud even. It was the fact that, for once in her life, she was the one that someone other than her kids needed, and she wasn't the one in need. De-De stepped in, bringing with her a cool gust of autumn wind.

The woman smelled of Amber and fresh laundry; her hair, with its tight coils, was braided into a ball that rested at the top of her round head, and the neatness of the hairstyle accentuated the angular bone structure of her face. "So glad you came," Kat said.

"Aw, thanks, I can't believe how organized you have everything now. Your place looks better than mine." De-De said as she took her shoes off by the door; and placed them onto the shoe rack. "I made chili with the recipe that you gave me," Kat said with the enthusiasm of a child. "I changed it to rid it of some of its spice, and it tasted just the way yours did. My kids love it, and it's impossible to get them to eat," she said, satisfied with having seemingly contained the contents of warmth and security within a single pot of chili.

De-De's fixed face morphed into a smiling one, "I just thought to myself last night that I want chili, take me to the kitchen, girl; I am hungry."

Kat placed her hand on De-De's waist, "Well, scoot over, and follow me" her small hands appeared even smaller against the fabric of De-De's oversized shirt as she pushed her aside.

When Kat made it into the kitchen, she reached far into the cupboard, pulling out four bowls, then the sterling silver spoons that were once her great-grandmothers. She lifted the top to the pot, which had been left on a low simmer since the early afternoon, and she swooned at the scent of spices as they stretched throughout the room. Cutting the burner off, she heard a gasp. Kat replaced the lid, remembering what she had done before the arrival of De-De, and made her way down the hall, turning toward the door to the left. She saw De-De standing near the stool and rope she too had previously once stood before.

"What is this?" De-De said, her large brown eyes piercing, concerned, and motherly. "I thought you were doing better, Kat; why would you…"

"I am, I am doing fine," Kat said, interrupting De-De. "I am doing great," "I just…. I just had to be sure. See for myself… I wanted to see how it would feel to stand near it."

"That makes little sense," said De-De, "What if your kids had walked in there? Did you do this in front of them?"

Her concern instantly turned to agitation. She suspected that Kat had fooled her yet again.

"You don't understand; several months ago, seeing that setting up that space like that, made me feel at peace because I knew it would be a way out. Now, where I am right now, seeing that makes me feel sick to my stomach."

"Feelings that the thought of dying never caused before in me. I am different De-De; I am turning into the woman I deserve to be. I just had to make sure. I wanted to make sure I wasn't just pretending. We both know how easy it is for me to…" Kat paused, "to Pretend I am fine."

De-De stood before Kat, whose face was red with embarrassment. "Okay," De-De said, "As long as you are good, that's all I care about. I still think you should take it down. You've tested yourself; you've changed. Take it down. Let's go eat some chili?" she commanded.

"Please don't worry," Kat said smiling. "I'll take it down; the kids are in their bedroom playing with the train set; do you mind telling them to wash up?"

"Of course! I've been missing them so much. I can't wait to kiss their little faces."

When De-De left the room, Kat reached for the rope that hung from the ceiling fan but stopped midway. She stopped smiling too. Her face, emotionless. Rather than grabbing the rope, she poked at it with her index finger and watched as it swung back and forth slowly. It captivated her, left her in a spell.

"What should I pour them to drink?" De-De yelled to her, breaking the spell.

"I'll get it," Kat hollered back and shifted her focus. Kat walked towards the door, flicked off the light, and shut the door behind her. Leaving the rope and stool just as De-De had found it.

After the children were put to bed, De-De read Kats short story. "I find your attention to detail fantastic; you outdid yourself," she said to her. Her brown eyes squinted as if it helped her process the words that Kat had written in her mind better.

"Well, I only wrote it the way I imagined it," Kat said, pushing her freshly cut bangs away from her round forehead, "I wanted to tell a story about a mother's love and innocence. De-De put down the papers she had been holding and looked up at Kat, "Well, this is it; you should submit it."

"What about you?" Kat asked, "Have you submitted yours?"

"I did," De-De responded.

"What's it about?" Kat asked, intrigued.

"Oh, you'll get to read it when I get pinned in the first place, don't you worry," said De-De, laying back on Kats' couch. "I'm curious to see what others have submitted. Do you think a lot of people submitted poetry?"

"Maybe, I was going to submit poetry, but then I wrote this story," Kat said, pointing to the stack of paper before De-De.

"I can't believe that Dr. Murphy canceled a weeks' worth of class this close to the end of the semester; she must be really going through it."

"I know. I heard she went to Argentina with her husband."

"As long as I pass this semester, I don't care what she does." Kat was staring up at the ceiling, twirling her hair around her index finger.

"What are you going to do after graduation?"

"I don't know," Kat said, "I honestly do not know; maybe I'll move away, find a job. I've been going to school for a long time, it seems, struggling; I can hardly imagine what it would be like to not have classes anymore. It's kind of been my identity, "Struggling, single mom, tries to finish college!"

The two of them laughed.

"We could take an end-of -semester road trip, all of us. With your kids. And I think after grad school, I'll become a professor like Dr. Murphy," De-De said.

Kat didn't doubt it. De-De was smart and would accomplish whatever she wanted. She was confident, determined, and had the freedom that Kat would kill for. This realization made Kat feel a sharp pang in her chest.

Nothing was holding De-De back, and Kat knew soon enough De-De would leave her behind in pursuit of a new purpose, a purpose far more important than she and her two kids. Their friendship.

"Yea, we should, that would be nice. A road trips! I've always wanted to visit the Redwoods. I've read that the sequoias get up to almost 300ft tall. It must be amazing to see in person." Kat's eyes were closed as she spoke with her head still tilted back, and De-De looked over at her feeling a wave of happiness well up inside her chest.

"Yea," she said, still watching as Kat imagined the great redwood forest, "We will go do that."

Kat hopped up, propping her legs beneath her, "Just look at it!"

Their tattoos were peeling and itchy, and Kat had already picked at hers. Its once vibrant blue hue was fading; a temporary dullness had made it appear worn and ugly.

"Whys' it look this way?" asked Kat, still picking at it. "You aren't supposed to pick at it; you need to put lotion on it," De-De said. "I got some in my bag."

Her fingers began fumbling through the miscellaneous items in her book bag.

"Here"

"Thanks, you know, I haven't been to AA in a while," Kat said, rubbing in the lotion that De-De had given her.

"Why'd you miss? Catching up on schoolwork?"

"I guess you could say that" Kat said, and then "Have you heard from any of the others since we got our tattoos?"

"No, I saw Emma at the library though, I didn't speak. She was with a girl."

The very next day, Kat made her way into the university library, where there was a flash sale, because the library was overwhelmed with both old and new books. As she walked around the library, looking at the stacks of books that were being practically given away by the low prices, she let her fingertips touch the book covers, and the binding.

The first section she stopped by was the table nearest to the librarian's desk. The lady looked up at her, blunt bangs, and serious eyes. Kat waved to her, feeling guilty; perhaps it was the look in the woman's eyes; it was speculative as if she hoped Kat didn't mess up the organization, or even worse steal.

At the table, there were numerous psychology books, ranging from "The Introduction to Psychology," "Narcotics and The Brain," self-help, and mind over matter books, and her eyes rested on a blue book titled "Circle of Stones: Woman's Journey to Herself", by Judith Duerk. She opened the book and flipped to the page her right index finger had rested on. The book read:

"Depression comes as a gift that stops one from hurrying briskly, confidently into the market. It stops one from rushing to the shopping center to buy one more bargain blouse for an already overcrowded closet. It stops one from emptily mouthing what one no longer believes in anyway.

Depression stops time.

……and one settles into one's own waters as a sailing vessel without wind…without wind…without momentum…and one sinks into ones' depths. And somewhere, deep inside, in the beehive tomb,

…. one has to step alone.

….and weeps."

She immediately closed the book; she knew she was going to purchase it. The words spoke to her, called to her from the page, and she needed to read more. When she made her way to the serious-faced librarian, the librarian's face surprised her by transforming into a smile.

"Will this be all for you?" she asked, revealing a wrist tattoo.

"That will be all," said Kat, "How much is it?"

The woman glanced at her, as if to study her, and said, "The children's books are fifty cents; the other one is free. Just take it."

"Really?" Kat asked, "Are you sure?"

"Yes, just take it."

This made Kat feel magical; she really did connect with the book and found it serendipitous that the librarian had chosen to give it to her for free. She quickly placed the book inside her bag, along with the others, and thanked the librarian.

Eager to dive into the text. It wasn't until late at night, after she had cleaned the kitchen, fed her children, and put them to bed, that she picked up the book again.

"But if a woman feels that another order in her life, she cannot relate primarily to her moments and her days. She becomes stifled and strangles. To feel alive, she must reclaim her life, moment by moment, as her own. A woman must break out of the old mold. She must risk disobeying given decrees."

This made Kat giggle, she had obviously disobeyed several decrees, but she kept reading on to pg. 44:

"Those dictated from outside as well as those written within her by her past. She must confront her internalized patriarchs and break out of the role of a good girl, a good woman that theft has scripted for her. She must submit to the dread that breaking the old commandments will bring. A woman must prevail against her guilt and be willing to suffer it as the price she must pay for her freedom."

Kat closed the book, digesting the words she'd read, finding it peculiar that she would stumble upon such a book, during such a transformative time.

VITA

She woke up with puffy eyes and for no apparent reason at all, thought about her monthly cycle. Despite the cramps she had been feeling, it hadn't come. Rolling over, she reached for the nightstand and quickly grabbed the scheduler she used for various things such as reminders and tracking her menstrual cycle.

Vita missed her period, and not only had she missed her period, but her breasts were also sore. There was only one explanation, yet she could not fathom the idea of it. Could she be pregnant with Grayson's child? The man she hadn't seen in weeks. It was when she shifted her two legs towards the side of the bed and let her bare feet hit the cool wood floor that a series of chills went down her spine. She experienced what felt like a dagger to her heart.

She and Grayson used protection and never went without. It was a circumstance she avoided like a plague, pregnancy, and the thought of being a mother sent a new wave of nauseousness throughout her body. She rushed to the bathroom, purging both her dignity and the lemon chicken she ate the night before. Embarrassed, ashamed, and frightened, she stared into the toilet bowl, the room spinning.

As she made her way downstairs and into the kitchen, she passed her youngest brother, who paid no mind to her red face and bloodshot eyes. He just barely moved out of the way as she brushed past him. Typical. Her mother stood near the stove, humming, the type of hum reserved for complacent homemakers and disappointed mothers alike.

"Mother," Vita said, feeling weak. Her mother turned to her with a smile, a warm one, much warmer than it had been all the years before. It seemed unnatural. "I'm making breakfast, you're right on time," her mother said, as she began to reach for the plates in the cabinet nearest to her.

"Mother, something is wrong, and I need your help. I mean, I don't know what to do," Vita said. She never imagined she'd be asking the woman who lied to her for her entire life for help, but who else could she go to, her father?

"Of course, what's wrong, and why is your face so red? Are you not feeling well?" she asked, placing a warm hand across Vita's forehead. "You are clammy," her mother said, her smile gone.

"Well? No, I am not well. I…" Vita stuttered; the words wouldn't come out, and without saying another word, she and her mother locked eyes. Vita watched as her mother's eyes turned downwards towards her stomach and then back up to her face again; she knew.

"I don't know what to do," Vita whispered as her mother pulled her over to the side, near the back door of their kitchen. Looking her up and down, she whispered back, "How do you know? I mean, you could just be …."

Vita interrupted her.

"No, I can't be anything other than what I am; I am not stupid; I know how this works. I've been a regular since I was 11 years old. Now I am telling you I don't know what to do."

"First, don't feel sorry for yourself, Vita; whatever happens if anyone can do it, it's you. Now what do you want to do?" she asked; Vita looked up at her with her large brown eyes, still bloodshot.

"What do you mean what do I want to do?"

"Vita, you've got two choices," her mother continued to whisper, "and I am not going to tell you which one to make, but you've got to think about who you are and what you want. You've got to think about what's important. No matter what you want, I am going to be beside you. You either keep this child or get rid of it," she said, knowing her family's culture was self-perseverance, at any cost. It always has been.

She took a step back; her mother had a certain coldness about her now; Vita swore her eyes turned black. That warm, inviting, southern charm, facade of a woman had evaporated the moment Vita hinted to her that she was pregnant. "Or get rid of it," her mother said without any hesitation.

"An abortion?" Vita asked, "I didn't even think of that."

"So, you want it, then?" her mother asked, her tone low and serious-like.

"Well, I don't want it, I just… I never thought about the possibility of. I guess I just… I didn't think you would support that."

"I support whatever you want. There's adoption, you know," Her mother said.

"And what? Carry it to full term; I don't know, I don't want it. I don't want Grayson. I didn't want any of it; I just applied to graduate school and a writer's workshop." Vita was feeling nauseous again, and her mother offered her a seat.

"You can carry it, carry and …."

"But then everyone will know mother, Grayson too, and you know him, he'd probably ask for a D.N.A test, demand that he gets custody……and if Daddy finds out."

"Well, if he wants custody, isn't that a good thing?"

"He would want custody of me! He'd want me to have it; he'd guilt me into it. And besides, how could I carry it to term and then just give it away? I…." Vita paused.

"We can't tell your Daddy, and you know that. Not unless you want it. You know he will want you to keep it, get married." tell your Daddy now, and

Her mother was now crouched before her, rubbing her thigh, leaving traces of flour on her bare legs. "It's the 1990's, times are different, you have options."

"Not very many, but options."

"I know," Vita said, knowing that if she brought anyone else into it, it would be complicated. "I'm not ready to give up my dreams, Mom."

"And you don't have too."

Her father walked in clean-shaven, dressed in a suit and tie. He had a way about him, always looked like he was on his way to a lecture, sermon, or a business deal. His blonde hair was graying and thin; his hooded eyelids gave him the appearance of a sleeping man.

"You two are up early," he said, glancing at the two of them who were still sitting across from one another. Vita's mother stood up, "I'll make your plate," she said, "you want gravy or jelly?"

Vita's father stood simply eyeing the two; he knew their way of being, and mannerisms, they were hiding something. Deciding to shrug it off and let them deal with it on their own, he answered his wife by saying "Gravy," and took a seat. Vita's anxiety increased; everything she had imagined for herself was becoming out of reach, the life she wanted to avoid more than anything was manifesting itself, and she knew a decision had to be made, and promptly. Time was running out. After she and her family finished breakfast, she helped her mother clear the dishes and stood next to her beside the kitchen sink; they had similar facial expressions.

It was at that moment she understood how daughters transform into their mothers, and how easy it is to become complacent. For once, she felt she needed her mother. Vita recognized that the coldness and sometimes complacency that she had sensed from her mother was strength, only expressed in the best way she knew how to express it.

Vita left home; she needed to go out alone, to think. Because it was early when she arrived at the park, there weren't many others around. In fact, she saw just one other person, a red-haired woman in a sports bra, biker shorts, and pink rollerblades. When she rode past, she gave Vita a warm smile as if to say, "You too?" and that is when the tears began to fall; the ache in her chest intensified. She felt her heart shatter, as she had let herself down.

DR. MURPHY

Dr. Murphy could tell by Bennette's posture and mannerisms that he had been having an affair with Summer. Locking the door to the hotel room, she leaned against it. How was it just two days ago she was making a lesson plan, and now she was in Argentina, one expensive effort to confront Bennette? *I needed to remind him where he belonged.*

Bennette would soon be standing before her within an hour's time, and she'd have to pretend she didn't know about the affair, hoping they could continue to pretend they should stay together. *Who am I kidding,* she thought; *I can't pretend anymore.* Finally, Dr. Murphy pulled her suitcase onto the queen-sized bed she'd be sleeping in, so that she could prepare for the night. Her fingers sifted through the various items of clothing, and before she knew it, she was thinking of Jo. *What is she doing at this very moment? What books has she read, and what type of music does she listen to? What type of woman is she attracted to?* These were those sorts of things Dr. Murphy wondered about while she did mundane tasks— it was easy for her to imagine what Jo would say, her facial expressions, or the way she'd look off in the distance when speaking about any subject she was passionate about.

Her curiosity about Jo had become her most favorite form of escapism.

Now, officially an hour after Dr. Murphy left the restaurant, it was time for her to get ready. She closed her suitcase and removed it from the bed. Dr. Murphy chose a canary-colored mini dress made of silk and paired it with green heels. The dress had thin spaghetti straps that sat on her shoulders and crossed at the back. It reminded Dr. Murphy of honey; the way it glistened and clung to her skin was sensual in more ways than she would be able to describe with words.

After a quick shower, she got dressed and sat in the recliner near the window, watching as the people below walked through the streets as if they were walking on air. Waiting for Bennette felt like an eternity, and she spent it in silence; it wasn't until she heard a knock on the door that she left the trance she had been in, and it startled her.

Bennette stood before her with flowers, Chrysanthemums.

"Thank you," she said, thinking ahead to when she would confront their marital issues.

"Are you ready? Bennette asked. "I figure we can go get some drinks, dance, maybe try some of the food we've been talking about over the phone?"

"Yea," she said, "Sounds great."

Stepping to the side, Bennette swung his arms in a sweeping motion as if to say, "Lead the way."

Dr. Murphy stepped forward, her canary-colored dress clinging to her form.

The two of them opted to hail for a cab, and it took them to the place that Bennette had chosen. There was an outside patio lined with soft white lights, mimicking the veins of ivy. The lights left a romantic glow on the backs and shoulders of the attendees while the smell of cigarettes and sweet red wine added to the vivacity of romance.

Bennette led Dr. Murphy towards a table that was pushed to the furthest corner of a balcony soon after placing his hand on her lower back. The two of them made their way through a crowd of people before finally sitting across from one another, a noticeable tension existed between them. Bennette clenched his jaw to keep from speaking too soon, and Dr. Murphy could not yet meet his eyes. It was the server that lessened the intensity when he asked them what they would like to order.

"I'll take a classic old-fashioned, with a cherry, please." Dr. Murphy said, not waiting for Bennette to order for her like he always had. Deep down, she knew she should not have ordered another drink anyways; her hangover was going to be killer. However, she needed liquor courage. It wasn't like her to show vulnerability, but she knew unless she showed any, she would have to face some harsh truths about herself. And that was something she wanted to avoid at all costs.

Bennette didn't take or add to her life, not really, but she would notice the difference if their marriage didn't work out. He took care of her most basic needs, sex, food, companionship. He was a commodity she had become accustomed to, like, a hot bath after a long day or mint chocolate ice cream.

"You know what? I'll take the same," he said. "Why not?" he smiled at Dr. Murphy,

"So, Bennette," she said, "I don't really know how to say this…. what I've been feeling, why I am here."

Bennette finally relaxed his jaw. *Had she discovered that he was having an affair?*

"I don't like to be away from you; the distance; it doesn't just seem physical; it's like we aren't connecting anymore. When was the last time we called each other? If we are being honest… be honest…would you have called me, had I not just shown up?"

She waited on him to answer but was only met with silence.

For the first time, their eyes locked. They looked through one another.

"Bennette?" Dr. Murphy asked, afraid of what she saw in his eyes.

The waiter walked beside their table and handed them their drinks.

"Thank you," Bennette said, finally speaking.

The two of them put their glasses to their lips.

Dr. Murphy took two large gulps and watched as Bennette sipped his own with more class than she was used to. He had changed so much since being in Argentina. His movements were slow, his responses direct, too calculated.

"I have noticed the distance too," he said, looking down at his hands which were folded, one over the other. "I always felt that you didn't want me close, August. Even when I proposed, it seemed like you had to talk yourself into it, into staying close to me. In fact, I was surprised you even said yes; that's how much I wanted you. I was willing to settle for only half of your interest. Half of your love."

"Bennette, that's not…" Dr. Murphy interrupted, but Bennette put his long index finger to his lips, signaling to her to be quiet.

"I'm not done, August," he said parentally as if she were behaving like a disruptive child.

This made her angry. Something about the way he signaled to her, and the way he sat there so calmly. The deflection, made her blood boil.

"You always make me feel like a burden, like I'm bothering you. Even when we make love, it's like you aren't there. Where do you go? In your mind?" He paused, watched her for a moment, and then continued.

"So, I take this job here, in Argentina, to give you your space. I knew that marrying you would mean I had to give you space. But I wanted this time to be different. I wanted to feel missed, wanted, loved."

Dr. Murphy straightened her back and leaned forward to get a good look at him. Her face was hot, and her heart began to beat violently in her chest.

"The last time I went home, you didn't even want me there. How do you think that made me feel?" His voice rose, and it was clear to Dr. Murphy that this was his attempt to stand up for himself, to detail all the ways she had wronged him, and gone against their marriage. It was his attempt at defending his cheating. His emotional distance from her.

She leaned back in her seat. If that was what he needed, to vent, then she would listen because, after all, she traveled all the way to ensure that their marriage was going to work. Never mind the fact that she already suspected that he was having an affair. She couldn't deny it; he was right about the things he said. She was distant, aloof, and had been for most of their marriage. Her contentment and commitment stemmed only from her needs and wants. Her need to have a routine, his emotional stability, the blind comfort he had afforded her.

"I am glad you came to visit me, and I love you. But I…."

"You don't want to do this anymore."

"No," he said, and at that moment, Dr. Murphy saw a flicker of light in his eyes.

"Bennette, I know things have been tough between us. I know about your affair."

She waited for a response. Bennette did not give one. He only stared back at her, unblinking. He didn't deny it, and it meant that Dr. Murphy couldn't deny it either.

"I know about your affair, too," he said back to her.

"I've always known, but I said nothing because I love you," he said.

"I love you, too. This isn't the first affair you've had, Bennette, let's be honest," Dr. Murphy said accusingly, denying the feeling at the pit of her stomach.

"And we both know, sleeping with a woman, its child play, it's giving, "drunk college student experiments with friends.""

"It's still cheating," he said,

"You may love me, August, but you were never in love with me, and if we are honest, the only reason you were so dead set on going through the motions all these years is because you are using me."

"Using you?" she said, the feeling in the pit of her stomach intensifying.

"Yes, you want something else. Something outside of marriage, hell, maybe you want marriage, but you never wanted it with me. In fact," he said, taking another sip of his drink, "In fact, maybe that's what you need; you need to find out what it is that you want."

"Or who. I mean, I hardly even recognize you, I've never seen you happier. You're practically glowing since I've left." Bennette continued, already finished with his drink, he signaled for another.

Dr. Murphy's eyes began to fill with tears, tears of embarrassment, rage.

"Look, if you want to go off and have affairs, sleep with whoever shows you any bit attention, and not take any accountability, that's on you. You can't gaslight me into understanding your decision to not work on this anymore… just because you want to be with Summer."

Bennette's lips slightly parted.

"I don't want you to turn this into a dramatic thing, I care about you and that will never change. I just know we aren't working anymore," he said.

"I've signed a new contract. I am staying in Argentina for an extended period. They gave me an amazing offer, and I think it's worth it."

"What the fuck?" Dr. Murphy whispered, "Have you just been plotting this whole time to never come back? A divorce? When were you going to tell me? How long were you going to just let me think you were coming home to me, your wife?"

"It isn't like that, don't make it seem like I came here with those intentions. I know we need to do this. For ourselves. I was going to tell you, and then you just showed up; I couldn't hold it in any longer. I am sorry."

The two of them sat in silence, yet again.

Dr. Murphy couldn't believe that she was sitting at a table with a man that could make those sorts of decisions with no regard for her feelings. A man that had the audacity to not only sleep with another woman but develop feelings.

Shame, she thought.

Her discontent didn't stem from the affair, the fact that the two of them had sex, not entirely, rather it was the fact that he wanted what they had with someone else, those mundane day-to-day and ritualistic activities that become muscle memory, routine. It was offensive that he desired to share the very comfort she had depended on for so long, for her own selfish reasons, with another woman.

"You're right," she said, finishing her own drink. She now held the cherry between her teeth and let its sweetness seep out onto her tongue.

"How do we manage this?" she asked.

"You mean, like our finances and paperwork?"

"Yes"

"Well, we both file. You can have the apartment. We never really shared finances. We each have our own insurance. I mean, if you really think about it, we've been nothing but roommates," he said with a large grin and chuckled.

He had found his way out in the only way a man could, by placing the blame on her.

"Okay," she said, "I'm leaving then. That's it."

"Okay," he said, reaching out to her with an open hand as if he was going in for a handshake. As if they had just completed a business deal.

Dr. Murphy stood up, "What about your things?"

"I do have to go back for a while to get my affairs in order, especially when we begin the process of our divorce, but other than that, I have very little belongings, don't I? Not anything you can't use or donate."

His words stung; he was right about everything he had said, even about her not wanting to be in the marriage; however, the casualness in which he accepted the ending of their marriage, or asked for it, still hurt her. It made her feel like a failure.

"I'll walk you out for a taxi?" he said, and she could tell from his facial expression that it came from a genuine place. She wanted to punch him, pull off her ring, and hit him straight in the eye with it, and for a moment, she was prepared to. *But what good would it do? I'm already embarrassed enough.*

"I'm fine, Bennette. I can manage." She said after folding her napkin, ignoring the hand that was still stuck in mid-air. She dug her heels into the floor and used them to scoot her chair back.

Finally standing, she straightened her posture, turned her back to him and walked away. She felt her feelings for him drain with each step, and in her mind, she had discarded them like trash.

A day or so later, when Bennette walked into the restaurant, the servers looked at him with judgmental eyes before quickly averting them. He couldn't put his finger on it, but the way they avoided eye contact made him feel as if he were the topic of conversation. He hadn't heard from Summer since he sent his wife away and really thought little of it until he walked into the kitchen and saw that she wasn't standing over the cutting table with a basket of fresh vegetables.

Summer always prepped and always had the restaurant's most used ingredients prepared, and yet Bennette saw no knives, no vegetables, only an apron. Her apron.

"Where is Summer?"

He asked the kitchen staff, who were busy organizing and preparing for the restaurant's evening opening, and when no one answered, he repeated himself speaking more loudly.

"Where is Summer?"

Everyone stopped what they were doing and stared at him.

"She quit the day before yesterday, sir," a waiter from the third shift spoke before looking down at his feet.

"She came in and left her apron. Said something about skipping town," his accent adding drama to the sentences he spoke.

This enraged Bennette, he hadn't heard a word about Summer's departure, and deep down, he knew that he would never hear from her again. He slapped his hands hard onto the tabletop.

"Fuck."

Suddenly, all he wanted to do was go home to his wife.

Summer was already ten hours into exploring New York City. It just so happened that at the exact moment that Bennette placed his hands on the cutting table in anger, Summer was placing her hand inside the hand of another man. One she met a few months prior, who offered her a good time under the one condition that she'd spend time with him in the city.

She kept their communication discreet on account of Bennette, but when Bennette's wife showed up, she called the man. Summer never wanted what Bennette wanted; he just assumed that she had. As a young woman, she wanted to explore, to learn, and she wanted a man that didn't belong to someone else.

DE-DE

Dr. Achebe was one of the few Black professors at the university and had come from Africa. He was sixty years old and always wore a suit with a bow tie, one with bold colors and blocky designs. His hair, like tiny white beads, was often clean cut, low to the scalp—which he would often scratch during his lectures.

Due to being considered an elective and offered only in the Fall, Dr. Achebe's class in African American Studies had very few students enrolled at the university.

"How "EEs" Eat Going?" He said to De-De with his usual accent, his I's always pronounced like E's.

"It is going well, Sir," she said, "I wanted to come by and ask you about the programs I am interested in; I don't know if I should go into teaching, go into a Ph.D. program, or go in a different direction?" She put her items down on the desk closest to his podium.

"I was thinking maybe an HBCU."

The professor was busy trying to connect the cords to the projector, at first only offering a series of grunts and nothing more.

Then he said, "What you have is an elephant," glancing up at her with a grin.

"An Elephant?" she asked,

"Yes, an elephant, and to eat an elephant, you must first cut it into tiny pieces."

"Here you are speaking in metaphor, and I am making important decisions," she laughed, "But are you saying I must focus on the important things? Can you be more direct?"

The professor straightened his shoulders. "That is up for you to figure out. You're a smart girl." Despite being frustrated rather than charmed, his words comforted her. She saw her own grandmother in the man's smile and in the kindness of his eyes.

It was true, she had decided; what was the point of panicking when she'd end up where she was meant to end up? There is one truth that she had recognized since being away from her family regarding her pursuits, and that was that things have a way of working out as they should. "God, and" she remembered her friend telling her once, "The universe always gives us what we need and when we need it," and the memory made her smile.

EMMA

Emma and Ruth spent most of their time together and were now trying to think of ways that Emma could exist in the world as her true self—a way to separate Emma from her mother and the church. The problem was, despite knowing what she did not want to be a part of her life, she didn't know what she wanted to be a part of her life.

Emma wasn't confident in the person she was to become and Ruth, who was both the main source of Emma's happiness for such a long time, had become her main cause of despair. The paradox was only causing Emma more confusion. It was a complicated situation.

Still, she and Emma came up with a plan. Emma would apologize to her mother and continue going to church and playing the role of a docile, perfect daughter just long enough to make it to graduation, and then she would escape. Otherwise, she'd be homeless, unable to complete her degree, at least that's what she and Ruth imagined, the very worst. Emma rubbed her shaved head. *A cardinal. A child playing across the street.* She stood in the exact room she had claimed she would never step foot in again just a week ago. As she stared out, her gaze extended beyond the trees in the distance, the mosquito-infested marsh, and the single sailboat that had been stranded there since she was a child. It was as if the world around her continued on while she stayed in place, heavy as a bolder, unable to move forward or backward.

Her eyes focused on the blue sky that stretched for miles and miles and the tree branches that seemed to move in slow motion against the wind. She soaked it all in, realizing the beauty that exists in simplicity, a beauty that is most recognizable when one is in solitude and silence. She, still not speaking to her mother more than was required, considered her escape. *Where could I go, and how could I escape?* Though she hated to admit it, her parents had done everything for her; her own independence went as far as driving to the university or hanging out with Ruth. She didn't know the first thing about taking care of herself in the real world.

Still, she could see herself walking the streets of a new city, wide and lined with trees. Cities that smelled like curry, carne asada, or maybe churros doused in sugar. *Could I be the type of woman that finds peace in a bustling concrete city? Maybe the mountains? Colorado. I'll have roommates or just one. I'll never come back.*

Emma tried to step away from the window before her knees buckled, it was as if her body was in direct conflict with her soul, wanting her to remain there and feel everything. Her body wanted her to do the exact opposite of what she had long practiced, the exact opposite of what they had taught her to do, which was to sit, and feel. Soon enough, Emma heard her mother's long skirt brushing against their wood floor.

"We have dinner with the Stewarts tonight, their daughter, you know, the eldest, she'll be here too." Her mother said to her, standing a few feet away from Emma's bedroom door.

"You will get along. I think she would make a considerable influence."

Emma's mother hadn't spoken a word to her since her return, and yet now, she was speaking to her in that fake tone. The tone her mother prescribed to people at church and other social interactions. The woman was a chameleon, a shapeshifter, and it was a skill that made Emma's skin crawl.

"I won't be attending that dinner," Emma said, looking out at the marsh in the distance again.

"Oh, yes, you are. You will join us, and you will pretend to like it. I've already told their daughter that you'd be here."

"Mother, I do not want to go," Emma said, still looking in the opposite direction of her mother.

"My house, my rules, and you do as I say until you graduate and go elsewhere."

In her mother's mind, she won, and Emma lost, because Emma came back home. Emma knew it too. Her mother had "won," albeit, and she had to do as she was told.

Clenching her jaw, Emma forced a smile. "You're right," she said to her mother.

VITA

Vita decided. Her mother called and scheduled an appointment for her at the nearest abortion clinic just three days prior, and now she walked into her daughter's room with hot tea. After sitting the teacup on Vita's nightstand, she opened the curtains to let the sunshine through. She stroked Vitas face.

Vita's mother never considered that she'd be in that position, to be the one her daughter confided in, to be the one that kept her secrets. Selfishly, she was grateful, and though the thought of having a grandchild warmed her, she and Vita both knew that Vita had made the right decision.

Vita was still a child, as far as her mother was concerned. She nudged Vita awake and gave her a moment to sit up in her bed before saying, "We should get ready."

Vita, wiping the traces of sleep out of her eyes, looked up at her, her big brown eyes had been swollen for days. "Are you sure you want to do this?" her mother asked, looking down at her with an unreadable expression, hands on her hips, their faces matching in expression. "Yes, I want to do it," Vita said, in the same tone as her mother that she learned to replicate perfectly.

It was just one hour later, and the two of them walked past a small group of women who held signs that read things like "Baby's rights, Give Life" and "Jeremiah 1:5 Love What God Created." A woman closest to the entrance of the building reminded them they were sinners by shouting out to them "Hell is hot." *Hell is where I'd be If I have this child,* Vita thought.

There were fewer than fifteen clinics left in NOLA, and she was walking into one of them. She was desperate, unable to imagine what her life would be like keeping a child she did not want. Inside the clinic, some women filled out paperwork while others stared off into space, biting their fingernails down to blood.

Worn out and dated pro-choice posters, depicting crying babies, women in caps and gowns, and 1-800 numbers clung to awful concrete walls. "Your future is important, and so is your choice," one of them read. Many of the women were there alone, with no one to lean on for support, but there was one woman besides herself that wasn't alone, one who sat with a man at her side.

The man appeared to be about sixty-five, while the woman beside him looked quite young, almost pubescent, hardly a woman at all. The woman's green eyes reddened as she fought back tears, ignoring the man who whispered into her left ear. She shrugged almost into a shiver each time he touched her and turned her body away. A discrete effort to separate herself from his presence.

It was cold in the clinic, a very specific chill that came not just from the temperature but also from the anxieties of the women, who, despite their decision, didn't know what to expect, nor knew how to act while waiting. For some of them, the visit to the clinic was both a funeral and birth, both an occasion of mourning and one of celebration.

A moment or so later, a nurse with thinning red hair, fine lines, and a smoker's mouth called her name. Her mother squeezed her hand tightly, one last gesture to remind her that she was making the right choice, a reminder that she, too, would have made the same decision for herself. She watched as they led her daughter back toward the procedure room.

Because she had been pregnant for almost three months, Vita, with the aid of the doctor, chose the more invasive option. *Still better than a coat hanger,* she thought to herself after learning about the affordability and legalizations of abortions in America. Of course, she did her research; if nothing else, she was a student. Afterall, Vita wanted to make sure that all the tissue would be excavated, so the doctor opted for an MVA, a manual vacuum aspirator. The procedure needed to be quick and precise as she wanted to immediately erase *its* existence from her mind. Vita felt alone and alien as she lay there, the plastic mat sticky beneath the weight of her flesh, her legs spread apart, and her feet lifted on turn-ups. A nurse named Linda did one final look over to make sure everything was as it should be and opened the door to let in the Doctor.

The doctor, tall and lanky, walked in with a pep in his step, a certain cheeriness that Vita felt inappropriate, considering the occasion. His face was covered with a mask. She inhaled and took a deep breath as the doctor bent forward, his body contorted into the proper position, and he did his job.

KAT

Kat put her hand in the water, checked its temperature, and then decided that it was warm enough. She turned off the faucet and stood straight up again. It was near bedtime, her children had eaten, and now it was time for their bath. It was only a few months ago that something as simple as running a bath for her children seemed too hard a task to manage, too draining, and now she was doing it each day like clockwork as if it were the easiest task in the world. She had removed the noose, too, the one that De-De found—-she wouldn't dare hang herself, not anymore—not with what her personal growth was beginning to restore.

It still amazed her; there she was, a *normal* mom, doing normal things and doing so without feeling so disabled by her depression. When her children got out of the bathtub and were sleeping in their beds, Kat decided she would pack her and her children's belongings, little by little, day by day so that after graduation they could drive away. *Westwards towards California?* After graduation, the world would be at their fingertips, and it would be the first day of the rest of their lives. In her mind, at least. Her apartment seemed too small, the cockroaches too unbearable, the neighbors and their loud music and "Hey Babies" too offensive, and she had had enough. She had outgrown her environment, and she decided she would leave, find a job in a new city, and give her and her children a fresh start.

The next morning, after swiping two travel maps from the filling station directly across from her apartment complex, she drove to the university and walked into the library. Once inside, she spread the pages of the two maps she stole from the filling station out onto the library table and smoothed them over with her small hands. After taking a deep breath, she eyed California, New York, Montana, and so on. How could she decide where to go if the only place she had ever even seen was New Orleans?

New Orleans—the city that wrapped around people like English Ivey or Wisteria, and she struggled to imagine a place that could compete with the magic that is within each crevice of the city, with its seashells and ancient-like oaks.

With her red pen, she put dots next to states she had always been curious about, Portland, Oregon for its mountains and massive trees, and Rhode Island because a character from one of her favorite books lived there. Maine. She felt a pull towards the North, and when she pressed her index finger over the New England states, she felt tingles at the pit of her stomach, deep down to the core of her. *Two roads, and I will take one less traveled.*

I guess I better start praying. She muttered under her breath before drawing a large circle around the specific location on the map. That's when she looked up and saw Dr. Murphy talking to the librarian. The two of them stood near the entranceway. Classes wouldn't resume until the next day, but Kat was happy to see Dr. Murphy, happy to know that she was okay, and they wouldn't find another note taped to her classroom door.

Dr. Murphy had spent the previous night packing everything that Bennette owned into cardboard boxes; she was determined to get rid of it all and had planned to drop them off at the nearest Goodwill. However, she left her wedding band on. She wasn't ready to tell anyone else about their divorce, nor did she think it was any of their business, and to have her finger bare, well, that would bring up a whole other series of emotions that she wasn't quite ready to address.

Dr. Murphy stood before the librarian, eyeing the curve of her upper lip, wondering how many other women at the university the librarian might have kissed. The woman was helping her find resources related to the magnum opus, "Tell Me a Riddle," which was written by Tillie Olsen.

In the book, Olsen writes four short stories that detail some struggles of women, be they familial or cultural, and Dr. Murphy could never forget the very first one, titled "I stand here Ironing." After confronting Bennette and accepting that their marriage was over the symbolism of the clown from Olsen's monologue had resurfaced and she thought the five would like it.

The librarian told her about a film version of the book that was released in 1980, and this made her very excited that she could not only present the text, but also use the film as a visual aid. *A little compare and contrast,* she thought. Dr. Murphy hadn't seen Jo or any of the students until then, when she looked over into the distance and saw Kat hunched over, making circles on a spread-out map. Even though she wanted to walk over and say hello, she didn't; she didn't want to interrupt Kat.

Kat had transformed herself, her skin was glowing, and according to the other professors at the university, she had morphed into one of their best students, a big contrast to how she appeared to them at the start of the semester. After requesting a copy of the film from the librarian, Dr. Murphy made her way to her office, where she shut the door behind her and plopped into her cozy office chair. It was one thing to feel a sense of boredom or anxiousness, but she felt it was worse to feel nothing at all. She felt dead inside. Earlier that morning, she looked at her reflection in the mirror and saw nothing more than crow's feet and deep lines that seemed to have crept from nowhere on her forehead. For the first time, she both felt and appeared to herself an old woman. Her marital problems aged her.

Grateful in that moment to be afforded her small office space, Dr. Murphy felt her body relax into the leather chair, her shoulders dropped for the first time, relieving the stress she felt on her neck. The semester was near an end, the season was changing, and so was everything else in her life, but her office, the chair, it stayed the same.

Just as she laid her head back, someone had slipped a yellow envelope beneath her door, and Dr. Murphy moaned as she stood up to retrieve it. Surprised, it was the result of a writing competition that several of the English majors had entered. Prying the yellow envelope open with her pinky finger she slid a folded piece out and opened it. It read: *"First place, "Getting Milk" by Kat Washington."*

JO

She existed in a constant state of maladaptive daydreaming during her overnight shifts at the hotel. It was almost 8:00 AM, fifteen minutes till, and the amount of coffee she had consumed had her wired. Maria, her relief, almost never showed up on time, and though it was something Jo was used to, it never stopped her from hoping. By 8:23, Ignacio, the owner's son, told her she could leave and that he'd monitor the front desk.

"Ay, she's always late," he said with his hands on his hip. He shook his head like a disappointed father, one that had given his wild teenager one too many chances——any hopes for redemption gone.

"Don't be hard on her," Jo said, "I heard she's got a sick kid."

"Always a sick kid, right?"

"Always a Dick, right? Jo replied while swinging her backpack over her head, almost swiping him.

"Easy, Easy, Josephina. It's difficult being a dick. You should take notes."

Almost two weeks since she last attended class, all she did was write, and she had written sixty-two pages in her novel so far. It was true that she had romanticized the pursuit of becoming a published author and had proclaimed herself as a literary genius, one with delusional confidence and unrealistic expectations, but she couldn't help it. She'd go into a sort of flow state and start writing where time would cease to exist, and the world around her would go silent.

Her physical needs were even subdued, for she had only recently survived on coffee, yet she bounced ideas around with such vigor. "Maybe you're right; see ya in two days!" she said to Ignacio, realizing that she needed to change clothes.

Once inside her apartment, Jo put on the same Levi's she had been wearing all week. It was grungy, she knew, but they were her favorites. *Who will know?* Dr. Murphy had been out for an entire week, and the only thing Jo could think about was telling her that she had started her first novel.

Before leaving her apartment, she poured more hot coffee into a travel mug and threw all that she had written so far, along with the doris davenport book, into her bag. Living only a few minutes away from the university, she had opted to ride her Catalina as usual and put her backpack on her shoulder before clasping the clip that wrapped around her waist. The crisp air–the smell of magnolias and Carolina Jessamine, made Jo fall in love with New Orleans even more, with each bike ride. *Is this what it feels like to align with purpose?* Jo's body buzzed with desire after taking a deep breath, almost in a meditative state. Her mind created images that reflected what would transpire in the next hour, when she would be sitting in Dr. Murphy's class for one of the very last times.

Once inside the classroom, Jo noted that there was a peculiar energy in the room. Everyone was in attendance: Vita, Kat, Emma, De-De, Jo, and Dr. Murphy.

Kat glowed; she had a certain look about her that told a different story than what it once told before at the beginning of the semester. In fact, Jo thought they all appeared different; it was interesting to see the metamorphosis.

The former version of Kat was almost undetectable. She and De-De sat next to each other towards the front of the room, and both were smiling down at the textbook before them. Without her nose in the air, Vita, usually known for her straight-backed posture, was hunched over, her skin taking on a bluish tint, which made her appear as if she was ill. There was a depth in her stare that seemed more fitting for the oldest version of Kat. Emma was happy; she had a very specific light in her eyes, one that Jo had never noticed before. *Funny, the things you notice when you pay attention. And myself, what about myself? How have I changed?*

Then, there was Dr. Murphy; had Jo imagined their connection? Unable to come to terms with the fact that they had not traded much more than literature—quick glances, and flushed cheeks, all the subtleties shared between two people who would never dare to say what they were really thinking. *She will never know what she's done for me, how she unintentionally kept my light from fading.* Jo knew people came and went, and that each experience led to another—*life is just a series of beginning and endings.* Yet, it hurt her to know that after the semester she'd probably never see Dr. Murphy again. That her memory would be the only place that a connection with Dr. Murphy would exist.

Jo walked towards Dr. Murphy, who was busy connecting the power cables to the television.

"I started a book," She couldn't help but blurt it out, it was as if she had been holding it in for too long, and it shot forward from her larynx like a dart.

"You started reading a new book?" Dr. Murphy asked her, understandably clueless.

"No, I mean, I am writing a book. A novel." *Why do I always sound like an idiot when I talk to her?* She thought.

"What is it about?" Dr. Murphy asked, genuinely interested. *You. Me. Literature.* Jo stood blinking at Dr. Murphy. Thinking.

"It's about life. Life experiences," she finally said.

"That sounds nice," was Dr. Murphy's only response, and Jo couldn't understand why she craved more. It had become apparently obvious the series of events, even the most difficult and trying times, which led her to pursue higher education, were leading her there. To stand before Dr. Murphy, all so that she'd be inspired—to write again, to *live* again. *Why can't it be more?*

Breathtaking, Dr. Murphy stood before Jo clueless about the impact she had on her life. She knew it was one of those moments she'd keep etched in her mind. Even though she had imagined the depth of it all, after all, that is what Jo did best. She assigned depth to even the most mundane, miniscule experiences, objects like rocks, books, and other things. She'd hold onto them and assign a sort of significance that the average person wouldn't assign at all.

Dr Murphy realized Jo wouldn't say anything more. "Okay, ya'll," she said, without acknowledging Jo's presence any longer.

That was Jo's cue, and she took it. Jo went and sat in her seat, a large lump in her throat.

Each of the women eyed the television screen with a similar type of inquisitiveness Dr. Murphy had the night before. The film, as the librarian said, correctly portrayed the same emotion and conflict that Tillie Olsen's anthology did. The characters in Tillie Olsen's anthology were women who were bound by things outside of their control, whether it was physical, emotional, or mental, and were eventually liberated. It was an anthology that celebrated transformation.

Emma, whose hair was growing back, looked defeated, and a part of Dr. Murphy wanted to go sit next to her, tell her it would be okay, yet how could she? She had no right and no way of knowing how Emma felt; it was all speculation. Besides, would Emma want that sort of attention? She always seemed so distant, so grateful that Dr. Murphy never called her name during the class.

Dr. Murphy's eyes then went over to Jo. Dr. Murphy knew it wasn't rational, to feel so connected to a woman she had spent personal any time with. A student, whom she didn't really know outside the confines of her classroom, or the literature that was shared.

Limerence—to long for someone, imagine something that isn't there. An involuntary intense state of desire for someone.

Dr. Murphy focused on the mole beneath Jo's collarbone. The skipped button of her gray blouse, and how the thin material of the shirt yielded to the rise and fall of her chest each time she inhaled and exhaled. Even in the dim lighting of the room, Dr. Murphy could see straight through to Jo's breast. Round, and she couldn't look anywhere else, and it was at that exact moment that Jo flicked her eyes upwards, directly at Dr. Murphy and at that time, neither of them looked away.

It was inappropriate, Dr. Murphy knew, and for that, she was ashamed. *This is the sort of thing they make movies about. "PROFESSOR GROOMS STUDENT," is what the heading in the newspaper would read.*

After class, Jo and the others picked through limp salads that were doused in too much dressing. They had never all eaten together at the university's cafeteria, and after attempting to, they all remembered why they never had. The food was nearly unbearable.

"Down to our final two weeks," said Kat, "Isn't it wild? I can't believe we are all graduating," causing Jo and De-De to join in.

"It's like I've been going to this university forever," Jo responded. "I can't even fathom that I won't have to come anymore. She felt that feeling in her chest that she sometimes got when she rode a rollercoaster or was on the verge of tears. It was a feeling she could never explain but always felt when she recognized that things in her life would change and that they would change quickly.

Jo still did not know what she wanted to do after graduation besides write, travel, experience herself more— learn who she was outside of those things which held her back. *Maybe I'll move somewhere where there's a beach.*

De-De, who had been having a hard time deciding what she was going to do after graduation, agreed with Jo and added, "I can't see myself as a teacher, but then again, what else am I going to do before figuring out what I want? Can you imagine me, a teacher or professor?"

"I'd love to be your student," said Kat, poking her shoulder.

Vita, smiling in response to the conversation, felt ill and excused herself from the table. The four women watched as she walked away. And before long, Emma and Jo did the same thing, leaving only De-De and Kat together. They both gulped down the rest of their salads in silence.

VITA

As Vita made her way out of the cafeteria, she felt dizzy. Ever since the procedure, she had had a series of panic attacks that left her winded and unable to find proper footing. Her mother attempted to assist her in any way possible, feeding her and allowing her to rest, but she didn't want to rest; each time she had a moment of rest or silence, she felt uncomfortable. Thoughts of what she had done, images of the child she didn't want, would pop into her mind as her imagination tried to combine the features of her and Grayson.

What would the child have looked like? Whose nose would it have gotten? The hair?

How could she have known that even if all of its tissue, any proof of its existence, was sucked out of her, scraped clean, she would still feel it? It was as if she still carried that mass of cells, the potential of what might have been, with her wherever she went, and this burdened her.

Once home, she walked past her family and walked into her room, where she sat on her bed and cried. Her mother, who had followed her, opened the door, causing Vita to look up at the sound of the creaking hinges. The two women made eye contact before her mother looked away; her heart was breaking for her daughter; she did not know Vita would take the experience as hard as she did.

It was what she herself had always wished she did; get rid of Vita as opposed to settling for a good family name and marriage. Vita's mother couldn't show empathy towards her because deep down, she knew Vita had made the right decision. She wanted to, though. She wanted to be there for Vita and show her empathy that her own mother was never to empathize with her.

She kneeled before Vita and placed her hand on her daughter's left thigh. Still looking down towards the ground, she said to her, "Vita, I know you are feeling so many emotions. Emotions I've never felt before. I don't know what to say, but I am here for you." What she *could* offer Vita had to be good enough, and it was better than nothing.

"You don't have to say anything, mother. There is nothing you can say. Thanks for what you've done so far." Vita replied, holding back tears.

Her mother stood up and plopped down beside her. There was an energy shift, and Vita was surprised at the amount of enthusiasm that showed in her mother's curled lips like she was trying to keep herself from smiling.

"Close your eyes," her mother said to her.

"I know you've been through a lot. I know you are doubting yourself and your choices. Give me your hands."

Vita searched for her mother's hands by feeling around, and when she found them, her mother turned her palms upwards.

"These are yours," she said as she placed two thick envelopes into the palms of Vita's hands. Because Vita didn't know what to expect when her mother placed the envelope in her hands, she scrunched her nose, and this made her mother laugh.

"It's okay, just open your eyes!"

Her mother squealed in delight. When Vita opened her eyes and looked down into the palm of her hands, a sharp pain shot through her chest. Her admission letters had arrived.

One was from Smith and the other from NYU, her top two preferences. She hadn't expected them to arrive as quickly as they did, and now that they were in her palm, she wasn't sure how to react.

"I think I should leave you alone for this, this is your moment, and you deserve it."

"Mom, we don't even know if I got in yet relax."

"You did. You got in. I'll be waiting for you downstairs to celebrate." her mother said and left the room. Vita sat in silence, still gripping the envelopes, almost too terrified to open them.

What if I didn't get in? And then, will I carry the guilt of what I've done for the rest of my life? It will have all been pointless.

Sliding her finger beneath the lip of the envelope to separate it from the glue holding it down, she pulled the first letter out. It was from Smith, and it took just a moment for her to scan through the words on the page and find the words she had been looking for, and when she did, a single tear slid down her cheek.

She got accepted. Vita's mother was right. And what Vita did was not done in vain. Vita reached for the next envelope, the one from NYU, and ripped it open with no hesitation. Accepted to the top universities for writers, the programs were prestigious, challenging, and competitive, and the acceptance letters represented all she ever wanted for herself.

It was worth it, she thought.

After standing up, she let out a loud scream and rushed down the stairs to where her mother was standing in the kitchen, putting frosting on a dozen chocolate cupcakes. She looked to the left and saw that her father and all her brothers were in the kitchen too. She fell into her father's embrace, allowing her whole body to grow weak,

"I got in, Daddy. I got into Smith."

"I know Vita. I knew you would."

Vita's mother stood behind her, gripping her shoulders, and comforted her in excitement. Her mother was living vicariously through her. Vita was well on her way to becoming the woman that her mother had always wanted to be, and it made her feel for the first time that she had made her mother proud, something she never felt she could carry out. It also made her feel empty inside.

She dared to let the intrusive thought work its way to the forefront of her mind.

Maybe if mother had looked at me like this before, before getting accepted, before the abortion, I wouldn't have felt inclined to get the abortion.

Just as quickly as she dared to accept the thought, she willed it away.

The abortion was her choice, and she is the one who would have to live with it.

EMMA

In the bathroom that was nearest to her room, Emma leaned forward to reach the faucet of the bathtub. After turning on the water and testing its temperature, she made her way to the shelf and grabbed her body wash. "Lemon, Eucalyptus, for a calm experience," the bottle read, "hmm" she mumbled and let out a small chuckle before pouring a generous amount into the now full tub. She watched as the bubbles grew, creating thick suds until she could no longer see through to the bottom, and then placed the bottle back onto the shelf.

Emma removed her clothing, a button-up blouse two sizes too big and her blue jean shorts. She reached behind to unsnap her bra before removing her panties. Standing there in front of the mirror, she recognized she had gotten too thin; *of course*, she thought, *I never eat.* And with that thought, she kneeled low to the floor for the tiny box that she had once seen beneath the sink. In it, there was a shiny razor.

It was so shiny she could see a glimpse of her reflection and use it as a mirror if she wanted to. Emma drug the razor against the insides of her wrist without pressing down and alternating sides. She felt nothing as she lowered herself into the tub and relaxed against the cold smooth texture of the ceramic. With one smooth flick of her wrist Emma dropped the razor and let out a loud yelp before covering her mouth. The cut started from the bottom part of her palm and ended in the middle of her forearm, deep enough that the warm water she soaked in turned into a soft salmon color. Captivated by the frosted flower design on the light fixture, Emma focused on the flickering light above her.

Dr. Murphy received word of what happened to Emma before any of the students. The dean visited her during office hours on Monday, and she could tell from how he entered the room that something was awry. He wasn't his usual self. When he entered the room, he didn't walk in as if he were trying to take up space, but he walked in like he wanted to make himself small, or at least feel small.

He sat down in the guest chair of her office and leaned forward before saying, "I'm sorry to say this, I know you got to know her very well because of your class size…but Emma, she is no longer here with us." Dr. Murphy felt saddened; she looked down at how the dean clasped his two hands together, unable to respond to what he had just said. Dr. Murphy did however always take note of how people reacted to grief or death, and in her moment of observing the dean, she recognized he was an empathetic man and that perhaps his egotistical demeanor was all an act. Perhaps he, too, like her, had learned early on that he needed to be performative to achieve all that he wanted in academia, and in life.

"What do you mean? Do you mean she died? Or that she just will not be in our class?" she asked, already sure of what he meant but hoping for it to be something else.

"She died. Her parents found her Friday night. It was suicide," he said, "And they do not know why she did it. They said she seemed fine the day before."

Emma wasn't fine, and what they didn't know is that after spending time in the cafeteria, she went to visit Ruth. Ruth's mother opened the front door as if she had been expecting a visitor, but her warm smile turned into a frown at the sight of Emma. It was obvious to Emma that Ruth hadn't told her mother about their rekindled friendship or about her troubles at home; she was a walking, living secret she felt, one that no one wanted to claim.

With a large smile, Emma greeted Ruth's mother and then asked if Ruth was available. Ruth's mother inhaled before exhaling and saying, "Ruth isn't here, and even if she were here, I wouldn't call her down."

This made Emma smile even bigger, "I see," Emma said, looking the woman in the eyes.

"Just one more thing," she said, "Thank you for not slamming the door in my face. If you could do me a favor, please tell Ruth I said thanks for the friendship and that I love her?"

Ruth's mother's face softened, "Yes, I'll tell her," she told Emma, while attempting to shut the door. This prompted Emma to communicate the last thing she wanted Ruth to hear, and so she blurted it out.

"Hope, too. Tell her to have hope."

Ruth's mother paused; lips parted.

"Hope?" she asked.

"Yes, Ma'am," Emma said, "She'll understand. Hope is the thing with feathers. That Perches In The Soul. It's an Emily Dickinson quote."

The woman nodded her head and closed the door, watching through the peephole as Emma walked away. When she turned, she saw Ruth was standing behind her.

"You should have let me say hi, Mom. I told you what she was going through."

There was a sullen look on her face. Her mother, who was now walking towards the living room, tied her hair up into a ponytail, "And I told you she is only trouble. You have too much going for you. Something isn't right with her, Ruth."

A day after she heard the news, it was Dr. Murphy's turn to give her four students the news. Standing before them, she watched as they each flipped through their notes, read or whispered amongst each other. Unsure of how to interrupt, Dr. Murphy cleared her throat, to rid herself of the lump that was forming there, and this caused each of them to look up at her. She had gotten their attention.

"I have something to tell you, and it's difficult to say. Emma, she's..." Dr. Murphy paused, "She passed away this weekend." The four of them gasped. Vita put her hands to her lips and felt faint. Kat and De-De hugged each other in shock, and Jo just stared at Dr. Murphy because she didn't know how to respond. There was a long moment of silence before De-De broke the silence, saying, "What happened?"

"I don't know the details," Dr. Murphy replied, although she did. That is when Kat stood up, upset, and rushed out of the room; each of the other women went after her and followed her all the way out to the dock on the lake, where Dr. Murphy had once taken them at the beginning of the semester.

When they made it to the dock to where Kat sat, their bodies formed a sort of "U" shape. Each of them sat in silence, looking out towards the water that glistened beneath the sun.

"I never got to know her outside of class," Kat said, "but I know this is where she would like to be. Sitting here with us. I remember how peaceful she looked when we came out here before."

"Yea," said Vita, "I just can't imagine how her family feels if I feel this way. I didn't even get to know her. Not really."

De-De reached out to Kat, and intertwined her arm with hers, pulled her close. Despite feeling saddened by Emma's death, De-De found relief in her mind. Something deep within told her that Emma had done something to herself, and it was all De-De could do but imagine the pain she would feel if it were Kat who had taken her own life instead. Emma's death had shown them all just how fragile the human heart and mind could be.

"I wonder if the family will tell what happened to her," asked Jo, "I mean, she seemed so healthy; she seemed like she was opening up, becoming who she wanted to be. It seems so odd that things would end that way for her."

Dr. Murphy looked over to Jo and nodded her head.

"Yea, she was just discovering who she was, wasn't she?"

Vita gasped and started stuttering.

"The," she said, unable to get the words out. All she could do was point, and that's when Kat and all the others saw it; a large butterfly that had seemed to appear out of nowhere was flying towards them.

"A butterfly." Vita finally said.

The four of them stood in awe, smiling as the blue butterfly landed on the wood railing. It stayed for just a second before flying off above their heads.

"You think it was a sign?" asked Kat.

"A sign of what?" De- De asked her.

"A sign that there was nothing we could do and that maybe Emma is okay after all, that we will all be okay…."

Dr. Murphy, who now stood at a distance, looked at them with a confused facial expression. *Have they lost their minds?* She didn't understand their reaction to the butterfly, but she was grateful, grateful that they somehow distracted themselves from the sadness they felt in their hearts. *Sometimes people must lose their mind first to find it.*

At Emma's funeral all four of Dr. Murphy's students walked up to the podium, holding each other's hands. They wrote a speech together, one that only Vita would read out loud. Emma's mother sat in the corner closest to Emma's casket; she couldn't contain herself and would let out a series of yelps each time Vita spoke about Emma's creativity or kindness.

"She made a big impression on me, on all of us, and we will never forget her," said Vita. Ruth, who sat next to her mother, kept her eyes on the ground before her, rubbing her ankles together until her mother tapped her on her leg, signaling to her to stop. That is when Ruth broke into a hard cry, too.

Her sobs resonated throughout the church, and the attendee offered her a tissue. She blew her nose into it, making her mother gasp in embarrassment.

"Dr. Murphy told us to write a letter to a woman, any woman that we admired. And we did, Emma. We each wrote one to you," Vita said.

The girls walked beside the casket. One by one, they placed their individual letters and butterfly trinkets into it. Kat and De-De's were pendants they pinned on Emma's dress; they each rubbed her nearly bald head before taking their seats. The pastor cleared his throat, making it apparent that touching the body was inappropriate.

Vita put a large butterfly stick on tattoo, still wrapped in plastic, in the casket. "Just in case you get bored up there."

"Or down there," Kat, the last to say goodbye, whispered before she placed a postcard that depicted a blue Morpho butterfly with its wings spread at the center of Emma's chest. "I found this one just for you."

"That will be enough," Emma's mother, just a few steps behind, said. A polite way of letting her presence be known. Kat glanced at her, irritated by the woman's showy hat and squeaky voice.

Emma's parents had arranged to release doves at the end of the ceremony. Each of Emma's family members, friends, and Dr. Murphy stood around in a circle before the pastor encouraged them all to hold hands. Dr. Murphy reached for Jo's hand. It was warm to the touch, pleasant, and the sensation of Jo's skin against her own caused her to feel flushed. She had wanted to touch Jo's hands, fingers, for a long time, and it was strange for her to feel such delight under the circumstances.

The pastor recited bible verses and referenced Emma's passage to eternity and unable to ignore the urge any longer, Jo rubbed her thumb along the outer edges of Dr. Murphy's index finger just as they released the doves. The two women stood next to each other in silence with their faces depicting sadness, but on the inside, the part of them that no one could see, they were like two pilot lights that had finally been ignited by a flame.

KAT

Kat already packed most of her belongings. She would use the money she had won from the writing contest to move, to start a new life, in a new city where no one knew her name. She had contacted a temp agency in Maine that assured her they could find her a job within a reasonable time frame. It was the woman at her AA meetings that solidified her plans.

The woman mentioned that she had a distant cousin who lived there, too, so the cousin and Kat exchanged phone numbers. The two of them seemed to get along just fine, and it only was a few days before the woman told Kat that she would love to open her home to her for a month or two just so Kat could get on her feet.

Using the rest of her financial aid for food and gas, as opposed to letting it go to waste, everything seemed to align; she had a place to stay, resources, and a budding support system all waiting for her, affording her a proper opportunity to create the life she wanted.

De-De, who opted to help Kat prepare for the move, now sat on Kats' bed, just like she had several weeks prior; she herself decided she'd go visit her family for more clarity about the direction she wanted to take in her own life. "You really did it," she said to Kat, who was bent over, going through a collection of records, deciding if she wanted to take them with her or not. Kat stopped what she was doing; she could hardly believe it either.

"I can't say I did it, you know?" she said with her hands on her hips, "I can't say that I did it until I am there and experience some sort of negativity. It is easy to be alright when everything seems to be going right, but I want to be alright even when things are going bad. De-De, I am scared."

Kat stood before De-De with her hands straight at her side. "You're going to be fine. I know you will. Do it for your kids, and for Emma. Do it for me," De-De said to Kat.

De-De agreed as she continued going through all of Kat's old records, too. De-De accepted to be a graduate student with Dr. Achebe as her mentor, and despite not showing it, the man felt elated that De-De had stayed at the University. "You're going to take my position, one day." He said to her when he heard the news.

"And you're staying here, right?" Kat asked.

"It's temporary," she said, "I just need time to figure out what I want to do, to save money. Since my grandmother died, it's been important to me to follow my heart and choose a path that will be most fulfilling. Right now, I am not sure what will fulfill me. "

"I get that," said Kat in response.

"It has been a wild ride, huh?"

"Yea, it's been wild for all of us," De-De said. Imagining herself as a tenured professor.

When De-De left, Kat made her way to her children's bedroom, where her children told her bedtime stories and spoke about the life they imagined having after moving away.

"There will be so many cool things to do," her son exclaimed, "Yea," her daughter agreed before falling asleep.

"Thank you, God, or, whatever. Whoever, helped me." Kat whispered into her son's hair before quickly falling asleep too.

VITA

Vita, who had been making plans of her own, preparing for Smith, sat on the front porch with her mother, the two of them swung in silence and watched as the sky turned from light blue to purple and pink, and then finally night. "Look at the stars," her mother said to her. "That you are fair or wise is vain."

Vita looked up at her in surprise; she had never heard her mother recite any poetry. "Emerson," Vita said, "Thy beauty if it lacks the fire, which drives me mad with sweet desire," and rested her head on her mother's shoulder. The two women looked onward, past their present moment and into the future, wondering what fate might bring.

"You are going to accomplish everything you could ever dream of," Vita's mother said.

"Everything I never could."

It was true; she would go to Smith and excel; she had to, or else the feeling that she had been keeping secret since her abortion would never go away. She was sure of it.

Vita hadn't heard anything from Grayson and wasn't sure that she wanted to. *How could I look him in the face without exposing myself?* She could picture it, her cheeks red and flushed, the precipitation on her forehead as Grayson eyed the length of her body. The thought of seeing him face to face made her shiver.

"Mom"

"Yes"

"So, do you love Dad, or have you just been pretending?"

Her mother's forehead creased; she appeared to be deep in thought.

"I do. I love him. I love him because he loves me, and I love him because he has never given me a reason not to."

"Do you wish you could go back and do it all over again? Even that night at the lake?" Vita continued.

Her mother sat up straighter and turned to look directly at her before speaking. "I don't think that I would change anything. No matter how it happened, I think you were meant to be here and your father to be my husband. I spent too much time thinking that my life would have been different but maybe all those things had to happen in order for us to have this moment. You are going to do something great in this world, Vita."

Vita felt a flush of warmth throughout her whole body. She had been waiting her whole life to hear that her mother didn't hate her, and that she hadn't ruined her mother's life.

DR. MURPHY

Many students were pulling all-nighters to study for finals and begging their professors for extra credit. They got their caps and gowns fitted as parents sent out invitations and planned parties. Graduation was but a week away. Dr. Murphy told the four women in her Women's Literature class they didn't have to submit their Capstone on account of what they had been through, but each of them did, anyway. They each gave them one by one at various times. The first to submit was Kat, who wrote her Capstone over Sylvia Plath, an analytical piece on how her poetry might help those who suffer from depression.

De-De wrote hers over Zora Neale Hurston, the short story "How it Feels to Be a Colored Me." In her piece, De-De detailed how Zora Neale Hurston's literature reimagines Black resilience and a Black woman's representation in society. Vita, after her most recent experiences, felt compelled to write her capstone about the essence of literature itself and how it provides women with a "room of their own." Jo, last, submitted a capstone that focused on Audre Lorde—the impact of her poetry and essays, as a Black lesbian feminist. Jo referenced text like, "Uses of the Erotic," and *Sister Outsider*.

For Dr. Murphy, it had been one of the most impactful semesters, and all she wanted to do was rest with hopes that her mind could find peace. Which in part had become difficult because Bennette contacted her several times over; he had plans, he said, to come back to the U.S. and talk things over with her. He wanted to go to counseling and work things out.

"I can't imagine doing the rest of this journey without you," he was saying again as she loosely held the receiver in her right hand.

Dr. Murphy stared off into the distance, breaking through time and space straight through to another life. She didn't have the heart to tell him, despite what he had done to her, the coldness in which he spoke to her that night in Argentina that she was content without him.

"I need time to think, Bennette."

"Come on, we both just hit a rough patch."

Rough patch? Rough years.

Finally able to get him off the phone, Dr. Murphy made her way through the stack of capstones submitted by her students, making sure that she left a personalized sticky note on each one. Afterward, she went through the last two stacks of essays and final exams from her composition course, glad to have finally completed grading. Dr. Murphy prepared for bed. No more assignments, there would be no more classes, the semester was technically over.

The violently quick energy that loomed over the university, professors, and students alike, was one that Dr. Murphy had been all too familiar with, yet, this time, it felt different. She almost felt she, too, like the students, was closing a chapter.

However, unlike her students, she had no plans, no idea what she wanted, only a glimpse of what she didn't want. She didn't want to be married, she didn't know if she wanted to stay at the university, and she didn't want to accept that she may have crossed an imaginary, one-sided, line with one of her students. It was hard to do though, to not think of Jo that way, to not imagine what it might be like to "experience" her.

If she allowed herself, she could close her eyes and take herself right back to the moment she and Jo held hands, feel that feeling in her chest, and relive the exchange of energy that left her with an aching need. If she allowed, she could again feel the heat of Jo's palm as it pressed against hers, and the heat that remained long after Emma's funeral.

It means nothing, and meant nothing, she thought, taking a deep breath to ease the butterflies in her stomach.

Dr. Murphy laid on her bed, staring up at the dusty ceiling fan Bennette always dusted. It disgusted her, she was disgusted with herself for not being able to remember to do even the simplest chores. *I depended on Bennette far too much*, she admitted to herself as she watched a tiny dust bunny float its way down to land on her bare chest. Dr. Murphy blew it off her, making it float its way towards the other side of the bed, still unable to shake the sudden feeling of loneliness that overwhelmed her. It was impossible for her to fall asleep.

An hour later she walked alone, and it wasn't until her mind finally caught up with her body's exhaustion that she stopped. *I've gone too far*, her footsteps slowed against the pavement of the sidewalk. She was concerned; everyone knew that the so-called pleasant neighborhoods were a hop and skip away from the so-called poor neighborhoods. The two were only separated by a few palms and gentrified areas that were bought, repainted, and resold as high class.

JO

Around the same time that Dr. Murphy lay staring up at the ceiling fan, Jo rushed up the stairs to her apartment, after she spotted a faint glimmer near her apartment door. The glimmer, she soon learned, emanated from a metallic-colored balloon that someone had weighed down with a rock and left for her. It was one of those helium-inflated balloons that people bought from the 99-cent store at the last minute. Attached to it was an envelope, and Jo immediately knew that her mother had left it for her.

When Jo pushed her way through the apartment door, she kicked off her Dr. Martens and ripped the envelope open, it read:

"It doesn't matter how long it takes; all that matters is that it happens. Love Mom."

A photo of the two of them fell out. Jo, about ten, wore a yellow dress with two pigtails that stuck out at each side of her head. The two of them smiled at the person taking the photo, proud like. Her mother's tight, high-rise jeans cut into the fabric of her plaid shirt as if they were painted on. Despite their disagreements and emotional distance, Jo's mother almost always knew exactly what to say. *Mothers were once just girls, and young women too.*

Soon after, rather than attending the early graduation celebration at Lafitte's that her friend Gary planned, Jo found herself with a glass of red wine and her back supported by four plush pillows. A little after 10:00p.m, she was nose-deep into a Flannery O'Connor book, a book that she had no intention of returning to the university library. It was a collection of Flannery O'Connor's best work, and Jo read each short story with gluttonous indulgence before flipping to one that was titled "The Daemon Lover."

The demon lover?

Jo read with eager eyes:

"… …. she had slept fitfully, stirring awake to open her eyes and look into the half-darkness, remembering over and over, slipping again into a feverish dream… … …."

The main character had no name, but Jo's eyes continued to roll over the text until the last paragraph. She stretched and twisted a singular strand of hair around her index finger.

The woman with no name spent an evening with a man who had agreed to return and marry her upon waking. The next morning, she found herself anxiously preparing for his arrival. She was happy, however the man never appeared. She had been stood up. The woman searched every corner of a block and knocked on many doors with each person or sign all sending her on another wild chase. Obsessed, she only stopped once she was sure to have heard him on the other side of an apartment door. One that she had never visited before.

"She knew there was someone inside the other apartment because she was sure she could hear low voices and sometimes laughter. She came back many times, every day for the first week. She came on her way to work, in the mornings, in the evenings, on her way to dinner alone, but no matter how often or how firmly she knocked, no one ever came to the door."

At the story's end, there was no real resolution. "That's it?" Jo asked after turning the last page.

To Jo, there was something so heartbreaking about the woman's perpetual hunt, her impossible pursuit of love. She slammed the book closed and tossed it on the floor beside her bed; betrayed, Jo imagined the woman knocking on another door. The woman's red and sweaty face, her watery eyeballs, bloodshot with disappointment. The characters in the books she read remained in her mind long after a good read. She'd wonder about their whereabouts or feelings as if they were distant cousins or some other person who she'd never see again, but somehow cared for. She knew that No Name wouldn't be any different.

Disturbed by the way Flannery O'Connor had chosen to end the short story, Jo flipped layers of covers off of her half naked body before making her way into her closet. In the dim light, she threw on an oversized sweater. The gloom that had arisen within her had become too suffocating, and because she needed air, she elected to take an almost midnight stroll.

It was cool out, and so eerily still in fact, Jo noted how she couldn't think of a comparable time. A time when the streets of New Orleans were as calm as they were at that hour.

Well, it is a weekday, she thought whilst passing a familiar street vendor who was packing up his caravan full of flowers—she decided she'd be a patron; Jo didn't want the man to end his night without a profit. The man's gold earring shone beneath the manufactured glow that lit the street as he gave her a blinding smile. His teeth were like white pearls.

"Two dollars," the sign read, and Jo stood sifting through a colorful bouquet of roses before picking a yellow one and bringing it to her nose. She searched her pockets for the two- one dollar bills she was given as cash back earlier in the day, but the man with the gold earring raised his palms up and motioned to her.

"No, No, you go," he said.

"You sure?"

"Yes, yes."

He spoke with a thick Haitian accent, his sincerity easier to discern than his words.

Jo twirled the yellow rose between her fingers, "Alright," she said.

"Piti piti zwazo fe nich"

"Piti piti zwazo fe nich"

"Bird, build your nest. Go."

The Haitian man spoke with both hands together as if he were giving a prayer and Jo nodded to show that she understood what he was trying to say. Despite not knowing at all.

"Thank you," she said, noticing the moon, a waxing gibbous, white, and swollen with illumination. Its milky glow sliced through the dark sky, proud to be the city's night light. *This is exactly what I needed, a nice walk,* Jo thought as she took the first few steps towards Magnolia St, and her heart skipped a beat.

There, across from her, on the opposite end of the street, Dr. Murphy stood looking up at the moon too. Her side-profile partially hidden by the shadows of the night.

Jo wanted to step forward, to call out to Dr. Murphy. To see the reflection of the moonlight in her eyes, but she didn't. What was there to say? Jo took one last glance at Dr. Murphy and turned away. A familiar sense of longing swept over her.

This book is dedicated to T.T.
To Baby, Sunshine, and Jupiter.
And lastly, to Carter and Milanna, and the time you lent. I hope this novel serves as a testament to go for whatever you want; despite. I chase my dreams so that one day you will chase yours.